Don't Wait to Be Called

DON'T WAIT TO BE CALLED

a collection of short fiction

JACOB R. WEBER

Washington Writers Publishing House
Washington, D.C.

COVER ART by Benjamin Faust

COVER PRODUCTION by Barbara Shaw

TYPESETTING by Barbara Shaw

Library of Congress Cataloging-in-Publication Data

Names: Weber, Jacob R., 1972- author.
Title: Don't wait to be called / Jacob R. Weber.
Description: First edition. | Washington, DC : Washington Writers Publishing House, [2017]
Identifiers: LCCN 2017027922 | ISBN 9781941551141 (softcover)
Classification: LCC PS3623.E39453 A6 2017 | DDC 813/.6—dc23
LC record available at https://lccn.loc.gov/2017027922

Printed in the United States of America

WASHINGTON WRITERS' PUBLISHING HOUSE
P. O. Box 15271
Washington, DC 20003

Contents

Acknowledgements

Grateful acknowledgement is made to the following journals in which some of these stories first appeared, sometimes in different form:

"American as Berbere" was previously published in *The Baltimore Review*.

"Everything is Peaceful Here Except for Missing You" was published by *Bartleby Snopes*.

"A Cinnabon at Mondawmin" was previously published in *The Potomac Review*.

"Silver Spring" was previously published in the *Green Hills Literary Lantern*.

I wish to thank the editors of all these publications for the encouragement they gave me by getting my first stories in print.

Thank you to Washington Writers' Publishing House for continuing the struggle to keep stories told only with words alive for local writers. Special thanks to Patricia Schultheis, Robert Williams, and Kathleen Wheaton for slogging through several rounds of revisions and offering intelligent suggestions.

Thanks to my brother Ben for taking my terrible directions for a cover design and somehow giving me exactlly what I wanted.

It's common for short story collections to "go together," to have common plots or subjects. These stories are the result of my disparate life, which feels like about twelve different lives coincidentally lived by the same person. I couldn't begin to thank everyone who helped me survive every one of those little lives within the larger life I've lived. I would like to thank: My parents who have alternately supported, encouraged, and humored the oddest of their five children; the Marines I served with who knew I didn't quite belong but accepted me anyway; the translators who were better than I was but respected my willingness to learn; Amy, who hears every story I write before anyone else; and Seamus and Keisha who first made me realize how seriously one must take the independence of characters, even the ones I created. Thanks to the Gaitskellians, the professors from Walsh University, my siblings, and every friend I've shared a long talk with; thanks to the instructors from University of Illinois at Chicago, where I tried to be a writer but wasn't ready yet. Thanks most of all to God, whom on any given day I'm 51% certain does not exist. If I'd have been more certain God did exist, I'd never have been able to write these stories.

Everything is Peaceful Here Except for Missing You

He causes his sun to rise on the evil and the good, and sends rain on the righteous and the unrighteous.

–Matthew 5:45

After hello, there are five phrases in Tigrinya you must repeat at least several times each in every phone call. None means anything, which is why they are so important to say over and over. Mama has hit them all at least twice. She's surprisingly adept at using Skype for a woman who never had a phone growing up or a computer until eight years ago.

How are you? Is everything peaceful? How is your health? How about your family? We are all fine here, except for missing you.

We use them back and forth, trying to keep them going like tennis students with a rally. The exact wording changes here and there:

"How are you?" she asks.

"I am fine," I say, then ask her back, "How is your health?"

"It's fine," she answers, then, "How about your family?"

"We are all fine, except for missing you."

Sometimes, we don't even answer the questions; we just answer back with another question. These are the volleys at the net at point-blank range:

"How is your health?"

"How is your health?"

"How about your family, are they healthy?"

"Is everything peaceful?"

"We are all fine here, except for missing you."

This is expected for us Eritreans; it's how the game is played. I've done it my whole life. It is as natural to me as it is for Haelim to twist and untwist her hair around a silver chopstick while she talks to her mother on her phone, pretending the whole time she doesn't live with a black man from Africa or have a child that is ours growing inside her. But I never even noticed this custom of ours until I heard Mohamed Idris speak with his mother.

A year ago, I was looking for a part-time job to go with the one I already have at my uncle's parking garage. A second cousin was stranded in Sudan when the guy smuggling him into Libya was arrested. It didn't matter than I'm still in college, or that I had never met this distant cousin. When a family member needs help in an Eritrean family, everybody helps. So I answered an ad for a Tigrinya speaker I saw on Craigslist that paid thirty-five dollars an hour.

The job turned out to be a contractor gig translating intercepted phone calls for the Bureau of Records. They were looking to nab Mohamed, an ISIS recruiter who wandered mosques, convincing young men their parents lacked jobs because they had disobeyed the Quran. He spoke Arabic, of course, but his mother was Eritrean, so with her it was all in Tigrinya. He kept his cards close to his chest, as they say, but they were hoping he was more open with dear old Mom.

When Mama and I finally get past introductions on the phone, we settle into the real talk. She burns incense next to her as she Skypes, because a home should smell blessed. She tells me that Cousin Biniam is doing well now, that he made it to Libya. He is waiting to find a boat to take him to Italy and needs our help to pay for it. He was working at an oil refinery near Tripoli, but then the revolution happened, and word got out that Gaddafi had hired an African army to protect him, so it wasn't safe for Eritreans to be on the street. There is nothing to say after that, so she asks, "Is everything peaceful?"

Mohamed didn't disappoint with his mother. They sounded so much like my mom and me, dragging out the greetings in Tigrinya. Hae-lim will one day speak to our child on the phone, maybe in Korean, maybe English. Nobody in our house will speak Tigrinya—that much I know. Mohamed's mother called him *b'ruh wedey*, my blessed boy.

When the Bureau of Records did a background check on me, they didn't like that my mother lives in Saudi Arabia. But my English was the best of anyone who applied, so they were stuck with me. We Tigrayans make a living all around the world from people who aren't crazy about us. My mother and sister make a good living cleaning toilets in Saudi Arabia for people who think of them as dogs.

When Mohamed was about to travel somewhere, he always let his mom know. She worried.

How are you all? We are fine, except for missing you. How is your health? How about the family? They are fine, except for missing you. I will be gone next week for a few days. I am meeting some people in Dubai. I will call you when I get back. Everything is peaceful.

In time, my cousin Biniam will drown with 318 other migrants in the Mediterranean Sea when their dinghy falters fifty miles from shore. A week later, Mohamed will go on a trip and will not call his mother again. My bosses at the Bureau of Records will not tell me what happened to him, but they will thank me for the work I did and send me my last check. Biniam's mother and Mohamed's mother will tell someone else that everything is peaceful, their health is very good, there are no problems, except Mohamed and Biniam are gone.

My mother says I am a blessed and bright son. I watch her on my computer as she brews coffee to share with my sister while she talks. She's had that pot with her in four countries. She tells me to be healthy, to be at peace. Hae-lim is a blessed and bright girl. May she be healthy; may she be at peace.

My mother and I always end our phone calls in Italian. We say *ciao*, one of the words the colonists left us along with the art deco government buildings. I was sixteen before I knew this word wasn't ours.

A Cinnabon at Mondawmin

Miss Kovac,

I need you to clean this up for me so it doesn't sound too ratchet. You made us read those two stories by kids from the hood who write the way we talk, but I couldn't get into them. I mean, I get that you want us to see ourselves in the stories we read, but I already know what I sound like. I know the problems I face. What I need to be reading are stories from people who don't have the problems I have. They must know something I don't.

So when I said "I didn't like that shit" just now, change that to whatever the right way to say it is. And take out all the places where I say "nigga." I don't really mind it, but I know you do. The first time I thought you were maybe alright was when you cried because we all called each other that. I mean, it was kind of dumb, because everyone knows us young black men call each other "nigga" all day long, and we don't mean anything by it. But you didn't want us to say that word, said it was a mean word and you left where you were from to come here because you didn't like people who said it. So I knew you were all right, even if you were a little simple.

So make this read the way it reads when you get done with your red pen in my journal. Make it sound the way people in Howard County where you live talk. Those are the people who don't have problems like the ones I have. I don't care if it's that thing you told us about the other day—appropriation. You said that was a fancy word for stealing, and there's nothing I have I wouldn't gladly let someone steal from me. Want my busted hairline I got because my cousin cuts my hair instead of a real barber? Take it. Want my bootleg Marbury shoes I got because I can't afford Jordans? Take them, too! Want my tired, dirty clothes I haven't had washed in a month, want the mother who can't wash them because her boyfriend took all the quarters? Want my brother's ten years up in Hagerstown lock-up he got for banking the guy who banked our cousin? Take all that stuff.

What you told us today when school opened back up after the riots didn't make much sense, Miss K, because the first thing you said was, "I don't want to hear anything about what you all did the last few days." I get why you said that. You're a teacher, and you have to go tell when you know we did something illegal. You just want to protect us. But you also put these notebooks in our hands and told us to write in our journals. When we write in our journals, you always tell us to write what's on our minds. Well, you know that what's on all our minds since we last had school has everything to do with Freddie Gray, with burning things down, with running from the police, and with stealing everything that wasn't nailed down at the Mondawmin Mall on Monday.

I was there, you know, at Mondawmin. I started over there right after school like most of us did, because everyone was saying we were going to march and take over the city from there. They were talking like we were Sherman's Army marching to burn down Atlanta. Yeah, I listen to some things you say. Everyone was talking righteous talk about a reckoning, and how our day had come. I'm telling you, we thought we were on our way to do a good thing. But the police were all over at Mondawmin. You couldn't get off the buses there. So folks tussled for a while, bricks and bottles, and I tried to see what was going on, but couldn't, and then someone said they'd broken into the mall, and if we couldn't clean up what was wrong with the city, at least we could clean up on everything in the Mondawmin Mall.

I admit, the first thing I thought of was getting some new kicks. My family acts like the decision for me to wear Marbury shoes is political, like we think it's criminal what a black superstar charges poor black families for shoes, but everyone can see through that. We don't even vote. So that big, white governor we got who just sent the National Guard here? Yeah, that's our bad, I guess.

Anyhow, I knew I wouldn't be able to get any shoes. The first place folks were headed was Foot Locker, and before I even got inside the mall, I saw all kinds of people running out with their hands full of shoe boxes.

Can you write this for me how I want it to sound, Miss Kovac?

Miss K, you're not going to believe me, but I went inside the mall and I didnt steal anything. I just watched. There wasn't anybody in there trying to stop anyone from stealing. People were fighting each other here and there over who got to steal what, but that was the only thing slowing anyone down. For the most part, as long as people weren't trying to make off with the same things, folks were actually helping each other out. I saw one guy put down his stack of stuff from GameStop long enough to help a girl who'd dropped what must have been about a thousand dollars' worth of hair. As long as you weren't competing for the same things, everyone there was all on the same team.

Would you believe someone was playing music? It wasn't the mall's music. They had turned that off. But people around here are creative, and somebody figured out how to put some Alicia Keys on while we robbed everything.

Okay, I've got to admit, even though I know you don't want to hear it, that I did steal one thing. But I doubt they'll send any cops to arrest me for it. When I walked by the Cinnabon, I saw there were some rolls still behind the counter. They might have been there for a little while, but they looked pretty good to me.

You'll probably tell me that stealing something small is still stealing, but, like Kevin Hart says, let me explain. I applied for a job at Cinnabon once, that same Cinnabon at Mondawmin. I needed to get some money for my brother's lawyer, and I figured I'd get to eat a lot if I worked there. I know you keep telling us that we have to stop eating all that processed sugar they sell to black people that gives us diabetes, but I love those damn things. But I didn't get the job. I guess that's good for my diabetes, but it meant I couldn't do anything to help my brother.

I'm not saying all this right. You have to fix it for me. You know we don't have a Starbucks in Sandtown-Winchester where I'm from, where Freddie Gray was from. All we've got like it is the Cinnabon at Mondawmin, and that's over a mile walk from my house. You think if we'd have had a Starbucks where we live that Freddie would've had his head slammed around in a police van? No way. He'd have been sipping some crazy drink with a long-ass name like you probably drink on the weekends in Howard County, and I'd have been making it for him. I'd have been pissed at him when it sent it back for not having enough foam. Instead, he did whatever it was he did to get himself thrown in that van. Don't look at a map and say, "but it's less than a mile from where he was arrested to the Mondawmin Mall." You know what a difference a block makes around here, let alone a mile? A mile away might as well be out there in Howard County, some place I've only heard of.

So Freddie is dead. They buried him, and then we all went to Mondawmin. I saw on the news how they were showing all the bad things Freddie did, saying he wasn't worth burning up a city for. But then that same news was making out that mom who slapped her kid around to be some kind of hero. If they had cameras in my neighborhood every day, they'd see moms beating up their sons like that pretty much all the time. I guess that means we've got no problems, because all our parents are looking out for us so much. She's no hero. I know that kid. If I had to bet on the one person I know most likely to go for a rough ride like Freddie Gray one day, it'd be him.

If she's a hero, then so is D'Andre's foster mom. She lets her boyfriend, who just got out of lockup himself, beat D'Andre almost every day. D'Andre is easy to beat on. You've seen him. He has to wrap his belt around himself twice to keep his school uniform pants from falling down. He only stays in that home because his sister is there, too, and he doesn't want the boyfriend to get with his sister. Which is why he usually gets hit. So I guess his foster mom's boyfriend is also a hero, the social worker who doesn't notice what is going on is a hero and the judge who put him there is a hero. Mayor Blake is a hero and the cops are heroes. This town is full of damn heroes. Sounds like a nice place to live. But it isn't. You know it isn't, Miss K. I know you care about us, but I also know you wouldn't hang around here after school is over. You get back to your house in Howard County as soon as you can. And I don't blame you. Why would you want to eat a Cinnabon at Mondawmin when you can have a latte at Starbucks?

Will you tell this right for me? I ate that cinnamon roll while I sat in the food court. I was the only one sitting. Everyone was running and excited. For the first time, we could afford stuff we wanted at the store in our own neighborhood. The sun was coming in, Alicia Keys was singing, and suddenly I realized it was spring outside. I bet I felt like you feel on a Saturday morning in Howard County when you grade our papers sitting outside at Starbucks. You must look around and see a wide open world and feel like you're free to do whatever you want in it.

Cinnabon used to be the place I failed to get my brother out of prison. This whole city is one big prison without a roof. But that roll was so sweet to eat there in the sunlight of the food court in the spring, for a minute it felt like I owned the place. We all felt like we owned something. For a minute, I remembered how you told me that Thurgood Marshall grew up where I grew up, and that seemed like something worth being proud of.

You've got to help me say this right for the people you know, the ones who see all this on the news.

When I finally had to leave, I walked home for miles through a burning city with icing all over my hands.

Brokedick

Standing in a row on a counter next to Chase were four foam phalluses, in varying shades of purple, mounted to a plastic display tray. They reminded Chase of stele lined up to meet the sun by a tribe lost to history millennia ago, a tribe whose sole remaining heritage brought busloads of European tourists to guess wrongly at their purpose. Periwinkle was for the completely limp dick, already leaning over on its own. Phlox was the penis that could get hard, but not hard enough for penetration. The one that could penetrate but not maintain erectness was thistle. Finally, the fully erect rod capable of satisfying an entire cheerleading squad, the penis the pills could give you, was a deep, throbbing, royal purple. Chase spring-loaded his middle finger behind his thumb and flipped the periwinkle phallus. It flapped back and forth in the stand. This didn't happen to be his problem right now, but it was good to know science would be there for him if he ever needed it. A toilet flushed in the room next door, followed by the sound of running water and a cabinet door squeaking open and shut.

Chase got up from the unbacked stool he knew belonged to

the doctor and paced the four strides the room allowed him as he took out his phone. He pulled up the web page on septic systems he had bookmarked. He was faking his way through a job as an insurance claims adjuster after also faking his way through the interview. His college job in construction had taught him just enough vocabulary to play the part. After he talked his way into the job, though, he was working with roughly a dozen other claims adjusters who all seemed to know every detail of how a building was put together. They were beef-necked guys with pickup trucks and three pairs each of steel-toed boots, guys who'd worked on their fathers' crews since they were fourteen. One woman, taller than Chase, with Matisse-red hair, could talk circles around him about 200-amp electrical service. Chase kept quiet, nodded a lot, and read like hell about anything involving construction. He invested weekends at Home Depot, next to young couples trying to fix up the baby's room, or desperate, middle-aged couples hoping that one more project on the cheap would raise their home value above water. The job was do or die, as they used to say in the Marine Corps. Chase was twenty-seven, and only recently out of his parents' house for what he hoped was the last time.

The door handle jiggled for a moment and Chase, feeling it was somehow wrong to be walking around, quickly sat down as the urologist entered the room. He then realized he was sitting on the doctor's swivel stool again and stood up as the doctor pushed through the door. He had a bald head and a giant gut, but he had a fearless way of talking. In boot camp, Chase had been the "scribe," the recruit responsible for taking occasional dictation for the drill instructors. He'd hated it, because the D.I.s talked too fast, and one was barely comprehensible, and they never waited for him to catch up. If Chase had tried to write down what the urologist said for the next three minutes, he'd have ended with a transcript that would have earned him push-ups for an hour.

Well, hi. Don't get up. I'm Doctor Glynn, and you're nervous. Well why shouldn't you be? Your dick's bent to one side and shooting red. Haw-haw and handshake. And what do you do? Insurance, huh? Oh, man, I bet you've been busy since Sandy last fall yeah. *Yeah it missed us but I know my neighbor and so on and how long has this been happening? Almost four years? Jesus, that long? How did it start? A buckling injury, huh? Peyronie's. The olllllllld broken penis. Well, let's get you to take your pants down and see if we can feel it and Oh, yeah, there it is right there and we're going to do this test and we're going to do that test and I want you to stretch it out just like I'm doing here, you see this? Not too hard, but I want you to stretch it just like this two hundred times a day. There's a tear in the shaft, see, there's a tear in the shaft, and I don't know if you've ever sailed—do you know what 'yaw' is? Yeah? Really? Well, the problem is like that. So here's something you can take and it's not really meant for this but some studies say it will work for Peyronie's so stretches and pills and I'll see you back here for the test next Friday. It doesn't feel great, I'm not going to lie, but it doesn't take very long.* And then the catch phrase *STAY AWAY FROM DOCTORS and haw-haw and gone.*

✦✦✦

The first time Chase heard somebody use the word "brokedick," he'd been in the Marine Corps a year, and Boss said it was something Chase wasn't. Chase was picking up cigarette butts outside the company office when Boss issued this judgment to Repkowski and the other dozen or so Marines in earshot. A brokedick meant someone who was too injured to carry an Alice pack on a hump or do pushups or who had a chit from a medic excusing him from something. The term carried with it the implication that whoever was hurt was malingering or just needed to toughen up. If your dick wasn't working, that made you a pussy. Marine Corps metonymy.

Clete Boss was no brokedick. Well over six feet tall, his head was topped with blond hair that curled up in tight kinks so he could break hair length regulations and never get called out on it. He had partied his way out of a basketball scholarship at some west Texas college. After that, the Marine Corps hadn't so much interrupted his fun as it had moved it to a new venue. During down time in the afternoons, as Chase's platoon of comms operators sat among the radios and canvas bags that smelled of mold, their legs dangling down from on top of a storage rack in the warehouse, Boss expounded on his adventures with the women of Oahu. The single mom who had orgasms silently, but with her mouth open, while her nine-year-old slept in the next room. (Boss pantomimed the face, eyes closed, face tilting up.) The short, chunky girl with all the piercings who put a saddle on Boss and rode him around her apartment until she fell over drunk and Boss put a pillow under her head and left her naked on her carpet. The sisters he'd somehow convinced to do everything any man had ever wanted two sisters to do with him.

If it were anyone but Boss, everyone would have known it was all bullshit, but when Boss was talking, you didn't question the truth of it. Boss didn't tell stories to impress anyone; he did it to entertain, to make others happy, because his life was the most interesting thing anyone in Alpha Company had to talk about. Chase owed Boss for the generally tolerant treatment he had received since joining Radio Battalion. Chase was in the habit of introducing himself by his rank and last name, as he had been taught in boot camp, rather than simply going by his first name among the other lower enlisted like everyone else did. Chase could feel the others beginning to see him as a square and possibly someone who needed knocked down a peg. In fact, he just couldn't help it. He'd gone by his last name since he'd played football in high school. Barfield was clearly a name, whereas Chase made people wonder if he were referring to a human being or something English lords did with horses and hounds.

Chase had played football because it seemed like the easiest way to avoid getting beaten up. Although he wasn't talented, he knew how to do what he was told, which was good enough to earn him a part-time role his last two years on the team. His playing time earned him just enough respect to roam the halls without fear. It was also just good enough to get a few second-string girlfriends, some of whom were even willing to have second-string sex with him. However, football also rewarded Chase with a herniated disk that the trainers were not willing to have treated correctly during the team's run to the state playoffs.

This same herniated disk became agonizing in the Corps when he humped a heavy radio on his back, and Chase found himself on profile with a chit from the battalion medics to get out of physical training. A profile was a dangerous thing, a ticking time bomb that, if left to explode, would fall in a hail of questions centering around his manhood. The term "brokedick" must have been murmured in union with his name at least once, because when Chase heard Boss's raspy voice float in with the fumes from the smoke pit that day that "No, Chase ain't no brokedick!" it had the air of an argument that needed to be settled.

Chase had once had the displeasure of trying to guard Boss during an intra-company basketball game. At least six inches shorter and lacking any of Boss's natural talent, he had allowed Boss to dunk on him repeatedly. The best you could say about Chase was that he was in the right place when he got dunked on. It must have been enough to exceed Boss's low expectations.

"You may not have great moves," Boss had told him afterwards, barely sweating and smoking a Marlboro from the soft pack kept in his sock, "but you've got a lot of basketball I.Q." Just like that, Chase was on Boss's good side. The timing was fortunate, because Chase's back began hurting him again the day after the game.

While the Marine Corps had its rigid and official rank structure, Boss carried an authority all his own. Officers felt it and respected it. This was a person chosen by fate to have life heed his wishes, and while some token adherence to the insignias of his chain of command was expected, it seemed obscene to insist that the obligation for Boss to show obedience to orders should ever be taken too literally. He would occasionally wear his green Wooly Pully with the arms tied over his shoulders and knotted above his chest, like he was on his way to a yacht club. Nobody ever questioned it. So when Boss insisted that Chase was not malingering, not a brokedick, the company naturally deferred to him, and Chase was able to hobble through four painful years in the Marine Corps, during almost all of which he was in a non-deployable status because of his back.

✦✦✦

Kelly always denied it, but Chase was sure she had first been interested in him only to cheat off him in British Literature with Dr. Kalamarkos. She was twenty, a sophomore whose first kiss had come when Chase was ducking sand fleas during boot camp at Parris Island. When she walked into class for the first time, Chase noticed her lips at the same time every other male in the room did, her lips that dove in around the top and bottom before they exploded out again, lips that offered up their implausible softness to be bitten by an unforeseen impulse. She had frosted highlights and had been through a string of the kind of men Chase would later hide his ignorance of gutters from. She was ready for a change, ready to *get her shit together*. And there was Chase, with his hair still cut short to Marine Corps regulations, because it had never grown back in right after he was out, sitting in the front with all the answers. She arrived early to get the seat next to him before the second class.

He hoped one day to bring Kelly to meet his Marine buddies at one of their reunions. She would be his proof that he hadn't entirely missed out in life on what they'd had the whole time they had been in the Corps; he'd just been a little late getting to it. Instead of having sex at the motor pool in the back of one of the Hummers, or hiding a girl in a wall locker when the unannounced health and comfort inspection came through, he'd had sex with

Kelly in the college library, up against the bookracks of the foreign language section, and they'd run together from the campus police when they'd been seen at 3 AM in the gazebo on the main quad. It was almost better than having sowed his oats with the rest of them, because while most of his Marine Corps buddies were watching the young girls they'd run with years ago turn plump and angry with their second and third waves of babies, Chase was just now getting to the good parts of life. It was like holding on to all your Halloween candy until the week before Thanksgiving, then laying it all out on the living room floor in front of your brothers to flaunt the virtues of your economy.

On campus, around people who knew no better, he became what he wished he had been in the Marines, what many of his friends had been forced to become. He told lies about Afghanistan, the places he'd never been too. He lifted weights at the campus gym early in the morning, and his back didn't hurt. He ate cheeseburgers every day and he drank strange concoctions of alcohol which made him tell more lies about what he'd done. He talked to Kelly about Beowulf and Germanic resolve in the face of inevitable disaster and he felt like a warrior and a scholar and a football star.

Near the end of the semester, the week after he had felt awkward receiving thanks from professors on Veteran's Day, Chase was sitting next to Kelly in her dorm as she scrunched her hair, stuck on her essay. He said something off-handed about *The Canterbury Tales* and some television show Kelly liked. He hadn't meant it to sound impressive, and he couldn't remember later exactly what he had said, but it must have seemed brilliant to Kelly, because she pushed her laptop aside and climbed on Chase. Those lips that everyone noticed were on him like fire and the two of them were ripping off clothes with such exaggerated passion it almost felt ironic. And then she was naked and on top of him and riding him wildly and it went *pop, pop, pop* every time she landed on him. But she bucked too hard and too high, and she slid off the end. When she came back down, his penis did not go back inside of her, but collided head-on with her pubis bone and bent hard to the left.

Before he even had time to think that he should hold it in, he'd already startled her with a scream, the kind he had been taught to use in boot camp to show he was not afraid. Then he was cussing, swearing at the pain, swearing at her for being careless, just swearing as though volume and variation of profanity were anesthesia. He clenched his fists as tightly as he could, and when that didn't slow the surge of pain, he punched the screen of her laptop, followed by the keyboard.

He knew while the backspace button was still falling back down from where it had ricocheted, knew before it landed upside down again just three keys away from where it began, that he'd gone too far. He knew before the campus police were in her room and he was being escorted out with his underwear covering his still-erect penis while a hall full of freshmen girls gawked, before he had to make a statement and hope that hers would account for the fact that he hadn't actually hit her, only her laptop—he knew before any of that that he'd lost his chance to tell stories to a crowd of admiring friends about how he had sex in a library with a girl who scrunched her fake-colored hair. He tried to apologize to her, later, during the five minutes before that last class they had together. But she had already gotten her shit together; she'd finished her essay on her own, and she'd figured out that the only wisdom he had to teach her was that most people are kind of lazy, so if you put in a reasonable amount of work, you're likely to end up okay. So it was over, and the day after he'd broken her laptop, a clot of blood came out when he tried to take a piss.

✦✦✦

On his second trip to the urologist, he went to a different room where there were no purple monuments to male virility on the counter, just a table to lie down on and a few informational posters with diagrams of the bladder on the wall. He leaned in to one with details in red and yellow of the male reproductive organs. Chase traced a line up the urethra and into the bladder, tried to imagine the line the scope would follow inside him. He hadn't researched the procedure the way he'd meant to, because he'd been working a night job in demolition, partly to learn more about construction and partly to make some extra money. The few hours he had to himself were devoted to sleep. He had only a dim understanding of what they'd be doing.

When the door opened, it wasn't the doctor, but two women there to prep him. One was a nurse, the other a student. Chase said he didn't mind the student observing, although he hoped she was only watching and not practicing on him. The experienced nurse sighed and squeezed past Chase to get into a cupboard. She pulled out something in plastic and opened it. She spied at Chase with one eye while the other scrutinized the syringe.

"You can go ahead and get undressed and lie down on the table," she said.

Chase didn't have enough room to take his pants off comfortably. He didn't want to face the nurse and the student when he took off his pants and underwear, but his only other option was to turn his butt to them, which had a rash. Chase opted for facing them and trying to remove his clothes quickly.

He was sweating when he lay down, and the white paper stuck to his butt and the backs of his legs. It began to rip beneath him.

"I'm going to insert a numbing agent into your penis now," the nurse said. She showed something to the student, who nodded her head. Both concentrated hard, consciously not showing any emotion, their mouths held a little too straight, their eyebrows furrowed as though in the middle of a nasty SAT question. "It's going to feel cold. It's going backwards, so it'll feel like you're peeing in reverse."

When the doctor finally arrived and put the scope into Chase's bladder through his urethra, it hurt every bit as badly as it sounded like it would. The doctor had tried his stand-up routine first, joking that the origin of the word "fuck" came from patients' responses to this procedure. But Chase didn't get the joke, and might have even responded obtusely that he thought it had a Scandinavian origin. He tried counting to thirty, but soon could swear he had already counted to 300. Things moved so slowly, he could have written down every word said with both hands. Even his thoughts slowed down so he could reach out and touch them as they went past, the way the family car had once seemed to crawl along the highway headed to the beach in the summers, highway markers seemingly hours apart.

One road marker. After the whole thing with Kelly had blown up, he'd decided to take whatever degree he could finish the fastest. He studied Spanish abroad in Mexico for a semester, finishing his electives so he could graduate early. The fact that it got him away from Kelly and a campus where he now had a reputation as the Marine with PTSD who'd beat some girl in the dorms nearly to death was a bonus.

Mile marker two. The summer after he got back from Cuernavaca, he'd worked 60 hours a week hanging dry wall and re-aggravated his back injury. He had a stroke of luck when the crew chief realized Chase could talk to the other eleven crew members, all of whom were from El Salvador and none of whom the chief could understand. Chase had a hard time understanding them, too. They spoke a dialect all their own, one Chase was sure was full of words only understood by the crew's eleven members, all of whom seemed to be brothers and all of whom seemed to be named Jose something or other. But Chase faked it and inferred what he couldn't hear. He ate pupusas with the Joses from the truck owned by their sister, and they all watched a Mexican telenovela on Chase's phone in the corners of half-built houses while they ate. The Joses were all impressed that Chase knew the entire story line going back to the winter, when he'd first arrived in Mexico.

They treated Chase like the foreman, and Chase was no longer able to hang a sheet of drywall for himself. The Joses were always ahead of him, smiling as they took one piece after another from the stack before Chase could get to it. Chase just drove in drywall screws and translated instructions to the Joses from the chief at base.

His last day on the job before going back to school, as Chase and the eleven Joses absconded for one last lunch in the corner, they indulged in sopapillas to go with the pupusas. Chase broke a sopapilla to share. One of the Joses said they were like Jesus and the eleven disciples.

"But there were *doce* disciples, not *once.*"

"I thought it was *once* plus Jesus, and Jesus made *doce*."

"No, there were *doce* plus Jesus besides."

"But then that makes *trece*. That's unlucky. How could Jesus and the disciples add up to an unlucky number?"

"Well, they were *doce* again once Judas betrayed them. Well, actually, I guess they were *once* after, because once Judas betrayed them, Jesus died."

Mile marker three. Last semester of college. No dating. No fun. Twenty-one credits to finish up all at once, then skipping the cold December graduation. Six months living with his parents after graduation, looking for work. Putting off a trip to the doctor to see why his penis was still bent whenever it was erect, why his semen was red-colored whenever he masturbated; the internet said that many buckling injuries got better on their own. His hadn't yet, but he hoped it would.

Mile marker four. It seemed to be shrinking as well as bending. This was unfair; Chase hadn't been blessed with anything like extra length to begin with. Googling "shrinking penis" had led him to a letter to an advice columnist from a man complaining of "micro penis." The man claimed he had never had a happy relationship, because it was always ruined when it came time for sex. He'd gotten more than one "awww" at the unveiling. The columnist's advice was to seek out someone else with a physical flaw, perhaps by looking at dating sites for people with disabilities. Look for other malformed freaks, you malformed shit.

The camera reached Chase's bladder and the doctor confirmed what Chase had been afraid of. The blood wasn't coming from the bladder. Chase's options were surgery to straighten the shaft or to live with it. The surgery, the doctor warned him, might also shorten him even more while it straightened. Chase decided to keep living with it.

He made up his mind not to dwell on it. He wouldn't waste his time wondering what might have happened if he just hadn't slipped out with Kelly. He wouldn't troll websites with chubby, smiling girls in wheelchairs or with bladder control disorders. He wouldn't even masturbate red semen into his hand. He would work. He took every claim he could get during the day, then worked every night in demolition, not even caring anymore if he learned anything, just wanting to work. His hands became worn down to grooveless ice rinks with a fine, yellowy, talc-like dust covering them that would not wash out. There was no longer any friction in his fingers, and pens would slip through his grip when he jotted down notes about accidents.

He earned a promotion. He no longer needed two jobs to work constantly; one kept him busy for eighty hours a week. The Amazonian red head started flirting with him. Chase ignored it.

A Marine Corps reunion invitation came. It was the fourth he'd been invited to in six years since getting out. They were planning to meet in Baltimore over Labor Day, because Baltimore was close to a few guys who had gotten government jobs after the Corps. They would stay in a hotel in the Inner Harbor, drink for three days and let the alcohol and the mood dictate the agenda.

Chase's first instinct was to skip it, say he was too busy, as he had every other reunion so far, but the night before reservations had to be made, he changed his mind and agreed to go. Maybe he could ask Boss for his secret. How could he be more like Boss? Command respect without asking for it? Have women without working for it? Have a goddamned twelve-inch dick that radiated authority, draped in robes of royal purple?

He tried to grow his hair out again. The last time he'd tried was when he got promoted, but it just grew fuzzy on the sides, like pubic hair, and before it grew long enough to try to style, Chase got sick of it and shaved it all off again. This time, though, he let it go for weeks, ignoring how it annoyed him, and it was puffy above his ears at six o'clock the day before the trip to Baltimore. He knew there was a no-appointment Neatklips near his office that was open until nine.

The minute he entered the salon, he realized something was

off. There were eight chairs to his left and eight to his right, all of them occupied by women. Heads that had been tilted down watching videos on phones suddenly turned up toward him, and glared with a dozen versions of "What are you doing here?" Chase froze, not willing to admit that he had wandered into the wrong place for a haircut.

"Did someone report water damage in the ceiling?" he blurted out. "I'm here from Smittsfield Insurance to handle the claim."

After half a dozen heads shook no, Chase turned to leave, exhaling as he pivoted, when a sing-song voice called to him.

"Chase? Is that jyoo?"

Chase contorted his torso in the door, his body half in the air conditioning of the salon and half in the late summer swelter of the early evening. At the back of the salon was a short, firm woman with coffee-colored skin, black eyes, and cheeks so fat they looked like they'd been stung by bees. She had stringy black hair that wrapped over her shoulders from back to front, one bunch larger than the other.

"That is jyoo!"

She set down the broom she had been holding, and something about the movement made Chase realize she was the sister of the Joses, the one with the pupusa truck. She looked different outside of her truck—still thick, but her skin looked clearer when not surrounded by steam and grease. She tromped sturdily on the tile floor from the last chair on the left of the salon to Chase. The way she walked reminded him of a sure-footed roofer. She only came up to his chest. Sofia—he suddenly remembered her name—took him by the arm and pulled him back through the shop to her chair. Her grip was unbreakable.

"Jyoo come in for a haircut?" she asked. Except for the accent on "you," she spoke clear English. They had always spoken Spanish at the truck, and it never occurred to Chase she could speak anything else. Her brothers were hopeless in English. He wondered how she had learned so well.

"No, not a haircut, I was just..." Chase started.

"Jyoo need a haircut," she said, getting out a gray apron. She reached up as far as she could to get her arms around Chase's neck and fastened the apron, pulling Chase down toward her head as she did. Her hair smelled like cilantro and mangoes, but the mangoes in shampoo, not from a grocery store.

Chase allowed himself to be pushed into a chair then lowered backwards, his head in a sink. She pulled a retractable nozzle out with a zip and started to wet his hair. She talked straight for most of the next forty-five minutes, almost as fast as the doctor had done. He struggled to keep up with Sofia's words, too. But unlike everything he had felt at the urologist's, her fingers brought him pleasure—the first pleasure he had felt from another human being in years—as she worked the shampoo down to his scalp. Her hands lifted him back up from the sink. Her fingers were not soft and delicate, but tough and strong, and they would have jabbed Chase if they were not covered by so much flesh. She pulled here and there at the clumps on the side of his head. Comb, bunch, snip, repeat. She touched his shoulders to turn him in the chair now and again. Finally, a ten-minute massage. She found the spot on his back that hurt, and worked at it doggedly. "Jyoo have too much stress," she said.

While she worked, she told him that she still had the pupusa truck, but she also had this chair in the salon that she worked a few nights a week. She was trying to make enough money to start a sit-down restaurant. She wanted her whole family to work together. Nothing fancy, she said. Just the same things she made at home.

"Isn't that a lot? The pupusa truck and then here?" Chase asked.

"Yeah, sometimes, but jyoo gotta work hard, right? To get what you want?"

"That's what I try to tell the people who work for me, yeah."

Chase asked what the bill was. She gave him her card. Her phone number was circled on it.

"First one is free," she said. She tried to wink, but her cheeks were so swollen it came out as a twitch.

Chase left her forty dollars anyway. "An investment," he said. "I want to eat at your restaurant." His back felt great.

✦✦✦

The next day, he flew into Baltimore and took the free shuttle to the Hyatt Regency in the Inner Harbor. They were supposed to meet in the bar, but the only two who had showed up by the time Chase arrived were Evans and Workman, two guys who had been at Radio Battalion before Chase's time. Marine Corps reunions were inexact—everybody got in and out at different times, so the overlap of any group was imperfect. Evans and Workman hardly knew any of the names Chase threw out at them, although they both knew Boss. Evans was a short, skinny guy with thinning hair, thick glasses and a thin moustache. He talked about

Afghanistan. Workman had a round face and talked about Iraq. Chase, who had watched all his friends go downrange without him because of his back, listened quietly.

Some of the guys Chase knew started to arrive. As each passed from the lobby into the bar, he would scan the scene, lost, until one of the gang lazily raised a hand to guide him. They talked for a while about the pranks they'd played back in the barracks. Chase never had realized it when he was in the Corps, but most of the jokes they'd played had been either homo-erotic or homophobic. Possibly both. One favorite game was to pull your dick out and say "Hey, look at this" to your buddy. Then, when he looked, you yelled "Meat gazer!" and punched him. There was also "tea bagging," which was basically waiting for someone to fall asleep and then putting your nuts on his forehead and taking a picture. They were a bunch of boys who joined the Marine Corps hoping to prove they were real men, and pulling their dicks out was somehow an important part of the metamorphosis.

Everyone except for Chase seemed to have put on at least twenty pounds. They drank Jack and Coke, because it was the drink most of them had learned to become drunks with in the Marines. They showed pictures on their phones of kids who smiled the same in every picture. Chase realized he had seen a lot of the pictures already on Facebook, and wondered why anyone had reunions anymore now that social media existed. Chase knew about half of the guys, but only knew Jenkins and Repkowski well. He noticed almost everyone watching the door as they chatted with him. Chase ordered a round of Jack and Cokes, including two for himself. He pulled out his phone, opened an article on dealing with tough employees, and wondered why he had come.

When Boss finally appeared, his face was flushed and sweating. His blonde hair hadn't receded an inch, and he sported white pants, a blue Hawaiian shirt, and a slight paunch. Chase immediately thought of Boss leading the platoon through a hundred flutterkicks in P.T. once and crying out "them's the fuck muscles" when everyone began to feel a burn in the lower abdomen. Boss must not have done any flutterkicks lately.

Everyone waved Boss over. The room instantly grew livelier. Chase could see years come off the worn faces of the fathers and husbands. The music in the bar changed from Lionel Richie to Jimmy Buffett. Drinks were ordered and machine gunned down, everyone buying for each other. Chase wondered how family men could afford a weekend like this, and it had barely begun.

By the time they left the hotel to head to the Bubba Gump Shrimp Factory for dinner, they were a merrily staggering platoon. Reno, one of the guys Chase didn't know, fell down as they crossed the bridge from the hotel to the pier. The platoon cackled happily. "Man down! Man down! I need a corpsman!" yelled Repkowski.

They passed a Hooters. Before Jenkins could even start his story, Chase knew what was coming. Jenkins recounted the night of Boss's bachelor party, a month before he went to Afghanistan for the second time. They had gotten a stripper, and one of her tricks was to put whipped cream on her breasts and charge five dollars to anyone who wanted to lick them clean. Although several of Chase's buddies had taken her up on the offer, at some point it became critically important to all of them for Chase to try it as well. They had howled and gathered around in a tight huddle, collecting $50 to offer the stripper to help Chase get over being shy about it. Chase remembered how loud they had cheered when he had blindly darted at her breasts, the terrible, sudden sweetness of cream and cool skin and acceptance. Boss had cried with laughter, his face so red Chase thought he was bleeding.

"Whatever we're doing tonight, I'm in it till the end," Chase muttered. A few heads turned to him. "Aw, shit!" Thompkins cried. "Chase is on the warpath tonight! Look out!"

***

He did his best to go toe-to-toe with men who drank for a living, men with body mass Chase did not have to absorb the blow of alcohol. They downed concoctions with names Chase didn't recognize—one was actually called a "Fuck Me Up." They left the restaurant hours later, no longer a discreet scouting patrol, but a mob intent on pillaging and destruction.

Chase threw up somewhere along the Harbor Walk on the way past the Hard Rock. But before anyone could yell "Man down!" Chase was back up, hands above his head, Rocky-on-top-of-the-steps style. "Blooh-blah!" he yelled, a Radio Battalion perversion of the Marine Corps' too-motivated "Ooh-rah!" On television, Marines are always saying "Ooh-rah," but in the real Corps, you get beat up for saying shit like that.

They visited a Karaoke joint, a reminder of an earlier night out in Okinawa. Chase picked out "What's Going On?" by 4

Non-Blondes and sang the whole thing in falsetto. When "American Pie" wasn't on the menu, the mob sang it anyway, loudly and badly, as a chorus and *a Capella,* arms draped around each other's shoulders. Leaving the place at that point was a mutual decision between Chase's comrades and the management.

A small group retired to the hotel after karaoke, but most were still with them as they hit the dance club. There were two different bachelorette parties at *Deja Vu*, easy to spot with the brides-to-be wearing veils and the maids in matching t-shirts. Boss was somehow at the center of both parties. Camera phones snapped everywhere. Every song was new to Chase, and, from what he could tell through the impossibly voluminous bass, they all seemed to be about asses. Chase watched Boss for one dance, then followed his moves exactly the rest of the night. A few bridesmaids who couldn't squeeze around Boss settled for Chase.

They lost most of the gang after that, but Repkowski and a few of the guys Chase didn't know were still in it. Boss suggested they hit a 24-hour convenience store, each purchase and quickly down a 40-oz malt liquor, then start a formation run down Pratt Street, with Boss calling cadence. Two of the guys Chase didn't know looked at each other with raised eyebrows. Everyone was wearing dress shoes, slacks, and collared shirts. To a man, they realized they were in danger of both injury and the extreme perils of the cliché of a night of Marine Corps binge drinking.

"I'm buying," Chase said, and ran across bleating traffic to the store.

✦✦✦

Chase had heard the advice "liquor before beer, never fear," but quickly couldn't understand on what evidence it was based. Maybe malt liquor wasn't included in that handy mnemonic device. He and Repkowski were side-by-side, with the two unknowns in columns behind them. Boss stood to the right, guide to their tiny platoon. They had only jogged a few steps down Pratt Street when he found he could not get himself to go straight. He wasn't sure if his body was failing to follow his eyes, or his eyes were confused about where straight was. One of the unknowns plowed into a parked car just as Boss had sung "two tons of titties and a loose brassiere…", and his buddy took him to limp back to the hotel as best they could.

That left Chase and Repkowski to zigzag down the road with Boss as the beer and fatigue broke over Chase like an anointing of oil. The trick to formation runs was that they were geared to keep most people in the run. As long as you weren't one of the slowest, you'd be fine. Chase had never seen the point of running in formation; forcing thirty people to run at the same pace all but guaranteed the run would be too slow for many, too fast for some, and just right for only a few. Running along the harbor, there were only three people in the formation. Three people in a formation was almost the same thing as a race.

They were all tottering. Even Boss seemed the worse for wear, and they moved slowly enough for Chase to right himself every few steps. The booze continued to crescendo. Repkowski seemed to be trying to stretch out the pace. Chase's back felt great, and he matched him. Lights were popping in front of him, leaving a trail of little dots streaming behind them. Chase ran harder and trusted the world to not get in his way. As Repkowski fell behind,

Chase heard him yell, "If you had run like that in the Corps, your ass would have been in Afghanistan with us!"

✦✦✦

It was just beginning to turn to dawn, and he was soaking wet. Chase was sitting up with his back propped against a bench. He was outside, looking at a large ship with old-fashioned sails. It was the kind of ship the earliest Marines would have served on, wearing leather guards around their necks to protect against sword slashes. Chase had loved stories of the old Corps, when men did what they wanted and asked no man's pardon. The kind of men who had enlisted while drunk somewhere, then served out their terms with honor when they sobered up, because what the hell else did they have to do? That was why Chase enlisted: he wanted to be a leatherneck.

Now he hated that he was at the end of a story that started with drinking too much. Every Marine had a million stories that started with too much booze. They had all joined hoping to become something else, and the only way to become new was to destroy the old thing. Alcohol was as effective a way to do it as any. It was more fun than the Taliban's way of destroying you.

He thought of Sofia, telling him that jyoo had to work hard. *Duro.* The same dual meaning in Spanish as in English. You could work *duro*, and something could be *duro*, tough. You could be doughy and soft, like Sofia, and still be *duro*. You could be bent down picking up dry wall and be hard.

"Where the hell are we?" Chase asked.

"On some pier, it looks like." It was Boss's voice, but Chase hadn't looked yet to see where Boss was.

"How the hell did we get here? Isn't that the *USS Constellation?*"

"It was your idea to come here," Boss chuckled. "I just followed you. And I have no fucking idea what that ship is. I'm just glad you gave up the idea of trying to board it last night."

Chase licked the salt and dirt from his lips. He felt his pockets. His wallet was still there, but his cell phone was gone. Just as well; he had probably jumped in the water with it in his pants.

"Where is Repkowski?"

"He gave up after he puked. He's gone soft."

A truck dropped newspapers in front of a restaurant across the street from the wharf and continued on.

"Come on, we better get the hell out of here before someone sees us," Boss said, and Chase heard Boss groan as he pushed his back against the bench and straightened his legs to stand. Boss's puffy belly jutted out as he stood.

"Hang on a sec," Chase said scratchily. "I need to take a piss."

As Chase stood up, his head retracted, and he staggered. He put his hands on his knees, his head down, and huffed for breath.

Chase looked straight into the harbor as he emptied his bladder into it. He was exposed here in front of the world but did not care. He held his broken dick in his hands, shriveled from injury, shriveled from being cold and wet. It was barely big enough for his fingers to get a grip on.

Maybe Boss was not real, not there behind him. Maybe he had died on that second tour downrange, the one when Chase should have been there. Maybe Boss was someone Chase had made up because he needed there to be someone like him. Maybe Chase would turn around and find himself alone.

Chase shivered in his wet clothes while he pushed out the last drops. It was so quiet in the city he could hear his own urine hitting the brown water. He felt that when he finished and turned around, it would be time to get his shit together. He shivered as he finished and did an about face. Boss was squeezing water from the bottom corners of his blue Hawaiian shirt.

"Man, that's impressive, Chase. You know the whole time we were in the Corps, I never could piss in front of anyone."

Chase finished zipping up.

Silver Spring

If Sufis in the desert had seen their own spirits made plain the way an American winter revealed them in the cruel cold of the morning, Daud thought, the whole religion might have been different. His hand had fallen outside the covers while he slept and numbness woke him. He whipped the blankets off the bed and added a sweatshirt to the two he had been sleeping in. He slid his feet, already covered in wool socks, into slippers and headed to Helen's room, trailing his blankets behind him. Her door was always open. She made him lock the front door of the apartment by handle, deadbolt, and chain every night before bed, but she kept her own door wide open. He crept as quietly as he could across her floor, although his feet were so numb he couldn't fully control them when they landed. The morning light leaking through the curtains revealed Helen sleeping with the hood of her sweatshirt pulled around her face, a face flecked with scars pink like American chewing gum against her dark skin. Her sweatshirt said *Howard University*, although neither of them had gone further in Eritrea than the eighth grade.

He spread his blankets carefully on top of hers and left the room. He passed over the bald patch of carpet in the hallway leading to the kitchen and thought he could feel heat coming up from the floor. He thanked God that the neighbors below ran their heat. Maybe he could pay them to turn it up more. Helen could convince him to freeze to make her happy, but she couldn't control the neighbors.

He sifted through the cupboards. They still had some of the instant oatmeal from the community food pantry. It came in different flavors: peach; maple and brown sugar; apple and cinnamon; and strawberries and cream. They all tasted the same to Daud: immensely sweet. The clock on the stove said 7:15. Every day of the week except today, they'd have both been off to the bus for work hours ago. On Sunday, she could sleep a bit longer. Forever, if she froze to death in her sleep. He probably had enough time to cook oatmeal on the stove.

She cited economy as her reason to keep the heat off, but Daud knew she was terrified by anything resembling fire. She could not be in the kitchen while Daud cooked, even if it was for her. When he'd first turned the heat on in the fall, she'd shrieked at the smell of gas through the vents. She was still too much of an Eritrean to skip coffee in the evening, but as she wouldn't heat the *jebena* or allow Daud to do it, Daud was forced to buy two coffees pumped from a carafe at the gas station around the corner every night and bring them home. So the traditional three rounds of the *awel*, the *kale'i* and the *bereka* were trimmed to one twelve-ounce polystyrene cup with a plastic lid. Daud wondered if she showered in cold water, then felt ashamed of himself for picturing her naked.

They had pretended to be brother and sister at the refugee camp in Israel so they could stick together. He changed his given name, Daud, into the Ethiopian version Dawit (at work in America, he went by David now. It was all the same thing.) His brother in Oakland had contacts in Addis Ababa who got him Ethiopian documents. It wasn't totally a lie to pretend to be Ethiopian—he'd been born on May 23, 1991, one day before Eritrean independence, so he'd technically been born an Ethiopian citizen. He had added "Gebreigziabher Tesfamariam" after Dawit to fill out his name, because that was the end of Helen's name. He had to have the most Christian name of any Muslim on Earth.

The Rashaida had captured her in Sudan a day before him. The Rashaida were ruthless, preying on desperate Eritreans. From Sudan, Eritrean refugees hoped eventually to make it to Israel or Europe, but the Rashaida were like grizzly bears feeding off the salmon run of the Eritrean exodus. Daud had heard stories about the risks, but when his third year of military service in Eritrea came and went with no sign of his being let go, the risks had seemed less important. He'd run into the Rashaida himself just across the Sudan border outside of Kassala. They took him to the Sinai desert in Egypt, where they'd dared him to run away.

"There is desert all around you," they said. "Anywhere you go, you will die in a day." They didn't even bother to set a guard most of the time. They said they would hold him until his brother in Oakland gathered the twenty thousand dollars to get him to Israel.

Daud warmed one hand over the oatmeal as it cooked in the

dented, donated pan. He blew on his other hand to warm it and felt his breath blow out the gap where his middle finger and half his ring finger were missing. The Rashaida had ways of getting families of refugees to pay up quickly, and one of their favorites was to make their victims scream on the phone while asking their families abroad for money.

Helen emerged from around the corner to the hallway, her skin looking bluer than her usual color, which had always reminded Daud of the acacia tree he used to climb in Adi Keyih. She looked at the stove top, the coils of the burner still glowing red after Daud had turned it off, and she scowled.

"*Haftey*, do you want some?" Daud asked. "It will warm you up."

Daud spoke to her in Tigrinya, although they were both starting to mix in more English. He sometimes got confused and switched to Arabic or Saho, especially if he had been talking to his brother or his mother on the phone recently.

Helen shook her head *no*. "You keep forgetting, Dawit. You're not supposed to eat before church."

Daud had tried to attend mosque in Silver Spring, but he felt his name was too difficult to explain. He was the first convert ever to change his name prior to changing his faith, and the second decision was caused by the first. His father had stopped believing in Allah during the struggle against the Ethiopians, and there were rumors that Muslims were not trusted by the government in Asmara, so Daud had barely ever gone to services at the Mosque back home, anyway. He had a Christian name, now, so he might as well act Christian, at least on Sundays. Medhane

Alem didn't seem that different to him from what little he knew of Muslim services. There were chanted prayers. There was the smell of burning incense. Helen seemed to accept the lighting of charcoals at church. Daud was happy just to be warm, although it would take ninety minutes of shivering at bus stations to get there.

Helen showered first, and Daud turned the stove back on while she was in the bathroom to warm his hands. He wished the International Rescue Center had settled them in Oakland with his brother if he was going to share an apartment with Helen. Nassir had told him it was never this cold in Oakland. He repented for every time he had cursed the heat in the desert.

Daud showered after her, and while he warmed up in the hot water Helen came into the bathroom to fix her hair. Daud heard her hands wipe the steam from the mirror, and got an erection thinking about the touch of her fingers, although he knew her hands were calloused from scrubbing sinks and toilets at the Renaissance Hotel downtown.

"You shouldn't run the hot water so long like that," Helen scolded him. "It makes mold grow, and it costs money."

He wanted to argue with her, but he couldn't while he was so hard. What if she threw the shower curtain back and revealed his secret: that he could no longer think of her as only a sister?

She kept fixing her hair for what seemed to Daud like a very long time. If she didn't want him to stay in the shower so long, she was going about it the wrong way. She was arranging her hair into *albasso*: long, high rolls that seemed like waves. She was four inches taller than him, a result of growing up reasonably well-fed in Asmara while he went hungry in Adi-Keyih. When she did her hair like that, she looked tall enough to be his mother, and he felt embarrassed waiting at the bus stop with her.

They dressed in their rooms, threw on every piece of donated warm weather clothing they had, and headed to the bus stop. She was covered in two scarves of clashing shades of purple and a blood-colored Washington Redskins winter cap with a yellow pom-pom on the top. It smashed down all the hair she'd just worked to fix. Her coat was a brown frock that was too thin, but at least hung down low enough to cover most of her legs. She hadn't found boots that fit her, and the wind bit into her ankles above her shoes and below the hem of her skirt.

She didn't emerge from the mass of wool twirled around her face during the long bus trip. Daud wondered what she might have looked like in a festive *netsela* made of silk around a bright young face instead of a scratchy piece of twisted wool keeping the cold away from her pulpy visage.

He'd never seen her with the face of a young girl, not even in pictures. By the time he'd been brought to the desert and stuck in the same camp as Helen, the Rashaida were already beginning to worry she had nobody who cared about her enough to threaten. In spite of having two of her teeth punched out to force her to give up a name, she still could produce nobody. Angry at having human livestock on their hands they couldn't take to market to sell, the Rashaida had set their most brutal captor on her. Daud remembered being surprised that the man the Rashaida used to enforce payment was so strikingly handsome. *Moges*, that was the word the man brought to mind for Daud. Gallant. Regal. He was tall and kingly, no blemishes upon his bright skin. There was another guard so ugly even the other guards made fun of him. Why was he not the one to torture the hostages? Why force someone so handsome to do something so ugly?

Gallantandregal made Helen call up an aunt in Asmara, the one who had taken her in when Helen's parents had been sent to prison, then treated Helen with such hatred the girl had resorted to selling her mother's wedding ring to pay a trafficker to take her to Sudan. While Gallantandregal flipped his cigarette lighter on and off on Helen's face, Helen's aunt insisted over and over she had no money. When Helen's screaming became too loud, her aunt hung up the phone and refused to answer any more calls. Gallantandregal pulled Helen's hands behind her back and spat in her blistered face. Then he set fire to her shirt, holding Helen as she writhed and squirmed. When she finally became too hot for him to hold, he released her, letting her roll on the ground until the flames were out. The back of her shirt melted to her back. That was Daud's first day as a prisoner in the desert. The next day, they were cutting off one and a half of his fingers as he pleaded with Nassir to pay them, for God's sake, pay them.

When they finally made it to Medhane Alem, Daud struggled to stay awake through the entire service. Helen was wide awake, it seemed, springing up and down at the right moments as though it was a dance at a *goyla* instead of church. He nodded toward Beyene in another pew when their eyes met. Remembering that they would have lunch at Beyene and Rahel's house after church,

Daud felt hungrier. He didn't know how Helen managed to seem so content when she had skipped breakfast altogether.

He couldn't follow much of the sermon. Tigrinya, one of the three languages he'd spoken in Eritrea, was the one he had the least grasp of. His mother spoke Saho at home and his father spoke Arabic. He only knew Tigrinya from the radio and school. He'd gotten better living with Helen, who, as a Christian from Asmara, knew only Tigrinya and a little bit of English. But after six months in America, his English was probably already better than his Tigrinya, and he'd never had much patience for sermons, anyway. It had something to do with Christmas arriving soon and preparing their hearts for the coming of the Messiah. He didn't understand. Hadn't the Christian Messiah already come long ago?

The food at Beyene and Rahel's was as vast and interesting as the talk was narrow and dully political. They had adopted Helen and Daud (Dawit to them) after their first visit to Medhane Alem. They were kind, served sumptuous dinners, and were generous to the point it embarrassed Daud. Most of the clothes he wore to work were from Beyene's collection. But Beyene was also a loyal member of the PFDJ, the ruling party in Eritrea. He narrated the one-hour "Voice of Eritrea" internet program every week, in which he railed in Tigrinya at the U.S. and its puppets in Africa. Today, as always, Beyene was scolding Helen and Daud, mostly Daud, for leaving Eritrea.

"You young people. In our day, we were willing to fight and die for our country. Your generation was supposed to continue the struggle by building our country in peace. But you are too impatient. You want a BMW, Nike shoes and gold watches, like you see in these American music videos. And you don't want to wait to build it for yourselves there, so you come here."

Daud was enjoying the spaghetti sauce, sopping it up with *injerra,* too much to argue. Rahel ran the Eritrean store next to the church, and she made equally great Habesha and Italian food. Daud was the only one who mixed them.

"I'm not saying that everything in Eritrea is perfect," Beyene continued. He wrapped *injerra* around the *shiro* in the middle of the table, then he put it on Helen's plate.

"Eat more, *gualey,*" he said, with a surprisingly gentle shift of tone before just as quickly switching back to scolding.

"Not that everything is perfect, I realize," he said again. "But it is your job to make Eritrea what you want it to be. Instead, your generation listens to promises of rivers of gold in Europe and America. You sell all you have to come west, sure that you'll be rich in less than a year. And what happens? What do you get? A few less fingers before they finally let you come and clean toilets for the rich? Last week, another five hundred of our young people drowned in the Mediterranean Sea, trying to get to Italy. The few who stayed alive by clinging to broken pieces of the boat, the Italians don't want."

Rahel finally cut Beyene off at this point by putting her hand on his shoulder and shushing him.

"What's done is done," she said softly. "What's important now is what they do from here on out. At least they have each other."

On the bus back home, Tupperware full of leftovers to take in his lunch that week, he wedged his half-finger into the carrying handle. Gallantandregal had hacked at random and carelessly left half his ring finger. A lost finger seemed like nothing to him in the desert. Of course he could part with it, if only he came out alive again to a better place. As long as he didn't die there. What did a finger matter, or an arm or an eye? He had mentally bargained whole limbs away in exchange for his freedom.

But after he made it to the camp in Israel, after realizing that his brother had really managed to find money and passports for both him and for the girl, he started to take jealous stock of the inventory of himself. The half-finger was only there by chance, but Daud tried to make it meaningful, a fortunate turn of events. He hoped that by training it, he could make his half-finger useful in ways his other fingers were not. "A beggar dreams what's in his own heart," his mother used to say. We all see what we want to see. He still had some movement in the stub.

What about Helen? What had she bargained away to God to be here now? That if God took her from Gallantandregal and his lighter, she'd never go near anything warm again? She had taken off her purple hat in the seat next to Daud. The hair that had been in neat plaited rows that morning was now ripped up like harvested sorghum.

A woman carrying bags that seemed as heavy as she was lurched sideways down the aisle. Her bags bobbed in front of and behind her as the bus accelerated and decelerated. When the bus changed speed, the bags would reverse and whack into her shins. She collapsed into the seat across from Daud and Helen and swirled her bags in front of her on the floor, still holding onto the handles. Her arms hanging down between her legs, she leaned back, and her flanks and thighs spread into the seats next to her.

She puffed out an exhausted breath, then, still slouched

against the seatback, asked, "You done your Christmas shopping yet?"

Daud turned to Helen. "*Intay ilatna, Helen?*" What had she said?

Helen explained about Christmas shopping, what the bags beneath the woman's feet meant.

"We cannot afford to buy presents this year," Helen answered the woman.

The woman's face turned from grape to prune. Daud knew the expression. Sometimes, black-skinned people born in America would address him like they were old friends but shut down as soon as they heard his accent and realized he was African-African-American, not just African-American like them.

It was even colder that night. Daud struggled to get to sleep. The coffee from the gas station seemed to jolt him awake more than the coffee his mother had made in Eritrea after dinner. He wished he had a cup with him in the bed. He'd have huddled up with it beneath the covers.

In the morning, he woke Helen before he left for the bus stop. She was able to leave an hour after him. He cleaned a college just outside the city, while she cleaned a hotel downtown, so her bus route was nearly a straight shot. In America, women cleaned hotels and were called "maids." Men cleaned large office buildings and were called "janitors." That's why she got to sleep an extra hour.

He pushed the cart for four hours from one room to another, gathering a hickory-brown can silently at each stop and tipping its contents into the cart. He spot-mopped sticky spots on the hallway floors. He used the side of his shoe to rub black scuffs off the tile. At noon, he met Mahmoud for lunch in the break-room. He heated up the leftovers from Beyene and Rahel's in the microwave. They tasted even better the second day.

"Helen is cooking for you now?" Mahmoud asked him. "That is good. You paid for her. You're still paying for her."

Daud explained that Helen had not made the food. He did not tell Mahmoud that Helen would not turn on an oven.

"Ehhhi. She should be cooking for you. She should be doing whatever you say. You bought her."

In the desert, Daud was given a phone and told to call his brother. They spoke in Saho, so Daud was certain his captors would not understand. He had just told Nassir about the girl he'd seen burned the day before because she didn't have anyone to pay for her. He'd only said it because he wanted Nassir to pay as fast as possible. But no sooner had Daud told Nassir about the girl than Gallantandregal smashed Daud in the jaw with an ammunition can. Who knows why he did it? Usually, the Rashaida didn't mess with the hostages whose families were on schedule to pay for their freedom. They were running a business, and if someone died, they lost their $20,000. Maybe Gallantandregal had Daud confused with another hostage they needed to prod a little bit. Maybe he did it just because he liked it. While Daud was still reeling from being knocked half unconscious, he was aware of a sensation in his hand. Something was wrong, but he couldn't determine what. He wasn't exactly in pain; it was something so severe it was beyond simple pain. He felt he should scream out, but more as an acknowledgement than a pure reaction. *Pay them.*

Pay them what they want. For God's sake, pay them. He heard his brother's voice in Arabic dimly coming from the phone: "I will pay! Don't hurt him! I will pay for both of them! Forty thousand for him and the girl, the one you burned!"

His brother thought the Rashaida were demanding payment for two people, and had agreed to it. If Daud had thought that he could let the girl die and save himself from having his fingers cut off, he would have. But Nassir misunderstood and paid for them both. That was how Nassir borrowed $40,000 dollars to pay for Daud to escape. That was why Daud would be paying back his brother for the rest of his life.

On the bus home, Daud dropped off to sleep and snapped awake every time the bus bounced over uneven road. He held his arms close around him and his knees up to his chest, partly to keep warm and partly as an instinct to guard himself. He was twenty-one, just old enough to drink alcohol in America if he had the notion, and already he knew exactly the measure of how fragile the human body was, how every inch of it had the potential to hold the rest of the body hostage with its own crises. You could make a strong man drop to his knees just by twisting his pinky finger.

Helen had arrived home before him and was straightening the cushions on the orange couch. *Sharmuta*. Evelyn was coming tonight to tutor them in English. All Daud wanted to do was pile everything he owned onto his bed, get beneath it, and sleep. Now, he needed to go back into the cold to buy coffee. They had to have coffee for a guest. On his way out the door, he asked Helen to cook something to go with the coffee, but Helen said she couldn't, there wasn't time.

"*Bejabi*, Helen. We can't give our guest coffee without something to eat. There is some popcorn in the cupboard. Just put the pan on the stove. It's easy."

"I have too much to do just cleaning," she said, and moved all the cushions she had just straightened again to make her point.

Evelyn brought a cake, anyway. She said it was called a fruitcake and that people ate them in America around this time of year. Evelyn taught them English by bringing movies she liked and playing them on a DVD player she brought with her. She pushed the buttons so that the words the characters were saying appeared at the bottom of the screen to help Helen and Daud to understand. She paused the movie every few minutes to go over what was happening. Daud hated when she did that. He'd rather half understand what was going on and keep watching the story than listen to Evelyn's voice, which was, like the cake, too sweet and fruity.

The movie was hard to follow because it had a lot of characters and they all spoke funny. Evelyn said it was a British movie, which was why they sounded so odd. Evelyn kept her coat and hat on. Daud asked her if she was cold, but Evelyn insisted she was fine. Daud said she looked cold and he turned the heat on anyway, but Helen said it was too loud and she couldn't hear the movie. At the end of the movie, all the characters went running to go tell someone that they loved them after spending the whole movie avoiding telling them.

When Evelyn got up to leave, she said she wouldn't be coming for a few weeks, not until after the New Year. She would be celebrating Hanukkah with her kids, and then she was going to visit her husband's family for Christmas. She had to explain Hanukkah, and then she had to explain that she had one set of holidays and her husband had another and they celebrated them both. She left the fruitcake behind.

Daud didn't always remember to brush his teeth before bed, but he brushed them long and hard that night. There were pieces of nuts stuck between his molars that he couldn't ignore. He didn't have dental floss, so he kept brushing and brushing until the piece that was irritating him most came out with spit and blood in the sink.

He was almost asleep when a call came in from his brother. Nassir wanted to talk about the boatload of Eritreans who had drowned in the Mediterranean last week, and the article he had written about it on *Antsar*, the Eritrean opposition website Nassir contributed to. It was Nassir's connection to the Eritrean opposition that gave him his Ethiopian contacts, the ones who had taken Daud and Helen out of Israel. Someone who was pro-government always commented on Nassir's articles, mocking him for being a slave to the old masters in Addis Ababa. Daud suspected it might be Beyene. Nassir always wanted Daud to become part of the opposition, to help bring down Isaias and his PFDJ thugs. Daud said he had to work.

"Daud, Allah did not bring you to America so you could get rich. You have to help those who are still behind."

"I'm not trying to get rich, 'akhi," Daud protested. "I'm trying to pay you back."

"Ah, yes, your expensive Christian sister that you bought," said Nassir. "Tell me, is she still your sister? You paid the price of two brides for her. Is she still sleeping in her own room? Are you still cooking your own food, buying your coffee at the gas station? Ha."

Daud said nothing.

"I still don't understand why you brought her with you from Israel. The misunderstanding in the desert was one thing. But once she was in Israel, you could have left her there. You had already saved her life. If she rotted in the Negev, that was nothing to you. Why did you make me get papers for her, too?"

Daud shook beneath his blankets. He clenched his body to stop shivering, but found that only made the shaking worse. He thought of Helen lying on the floor of the tent, melted bits of shirt stuck to her back. He had tried to encourage her, but nothing seemed right. There didn't seem to be anything he could do. They had nothing in common, save mistreatment at the hands of the same people.

"I did it because the people who cut my fingers off wouldn't have done it."

Daud could not get to sleep. He should have bought one of the electric blankets that Mahmoud had told him about. He thought it was too much money last week, but now he'd have gladly exchanged that forty dollars to be warm. Nassir could yell all he wanted about Daud shorting him with his weekly installment.

Daud gave up trying to sleep and wandered the hallway between his room and the living room, passing the kitchen, the bathroom and Helen's room as he went. Her breathing was barely audible. She'd make a good wife to someone, she slept so quietly. He'd never heard her snore.

When walking the floor failed to warm him up, he flicked the burner on the stove and cupped his hands around it. His patience with Helen was running out. He understood if she had promised God, lying crumpled on the floor of the hostages' tent in the Sinai, that if He took her out of there she would never go near fire again, or whatever wild promise she had made. But she was here now. Whatever God had not taken from them in the desert was implicitly theirs to keep.

He started to warm up, fell asleep standing, then jumped awake when he let his hands drop and his left hand fell onto the burner. His pinky and his ring finger stub had stuck to the burner for a second. When he pulled them off, a chunk of his own flesh lay burning on the coils.

"*Sharmuta!*" he cursed.

He cranked on the faucet of the kitchen sink and jabbed his hand under the cold water. Immediately, he felt his whole body start to shiver again, and he cursed repeatedly, now directing it more at Helen than at the burner. This was too much. He swaddled his hand in a bread wrapper he pulled from the trash and headed toward Helen's room. He yanked the covers back from on top of her and she sprang to a sitting position.

"What are you doing?" she barked at him. She had spoken in English. Awakened from a dead sleep, and her instinct had been to burst out in English.

"I am cold, *baftey*," Daud said.

"Then put on more clothes."

"I am wearing everything I can put on. My hand is burnt. Let me turn the heat on or I am coming in there with you."

"You can't, Daud. You promised. You promised we'd be like brother and sister."

"I am so cold, Helen. And I burned my hand."

"You shouldn't have turned the stove on."

"Maybe, but it still hurts. And I am freezing."

Daud could not stand any longer, his hand throbbing from heat and cold. He slid over the mountain of blankets, turned on his side next to Helen, and pulled the mountain back over them both.

"David!"

But Daud only shook in the bed next to her, saying nothing. He did not put his arm around Helen, or press his raging erection next to her. He had not come running to her in an airport to tell her that he loved her. But he had made a small advance to a position from which he would not retreat.

Whether from pity or just fatigue, she lay back down, facing away from him. They were both wrapped in layers of bulky clothing, hoods over their heads. Daud stuffed his burned hand between his thighs and waited for Helen's heat to come to him.

At work the next day, Mahmoud told him that last night had been a record low temperature. Homeless people died on nights like that one. They were in the middle of a cold streak that would last for days, all the way up to Christmas.

There was extra work, if Daud wanted it, which he did, of course. He and Mahmoud spent evenings buffing floors while the students were on break. He didn't make it back to the apartment until very late. He switched the coffee he bought at the gas station to decaffeinated, but didn't tell Helen. She seemed to enjoy it as always. He continued to sleep in her room, in her bed, next to her. They never touched, but they stayed close enough to keep warm. She was so tall, Daud thought as he lay next to her. *Encheyti*, she'd have been called in romantic songs in Eritrea. A tree.

Work let him go early on Christmas Eve. He had forgotten what it was like riding the bus in the daylight. They pulled up to the mall at Ellsworth Place, and a cluster of passengers got on, carrying bags. He got an idea as sudden and unmistakable as the stove burn. He jumped from his seat and shouted for the bus to stop, not realizing that it was still motionless.

When he returned to the apartment, Helen was not in the living room, and he quickly snuck over to the couch. He pulled the couch away from the wall and stuffed a large box behind. He left the apartment, shouting back toward Helen's room that he was going to get coffee. She answered something muffled. She had probably been sleeping. The hallways smelled of old curry.

He bought regular coffee this time instead of decaf. He also bought some instant popcorn in a vacuum-sealed bag. He left a dollar in the tip jar of the man behind the counter. He had never left a tip before. He told the man Merry Christmas.

He presented his gift to Helen while serving her the coffee. It was a small microwave oven. Daud had put a red bow on top. He showed her the bag of popcorn.

"We can heat it in here. You don't have to use the stove. You can heat all kinds of things in it."

The scars on her face turned from pink to dark, or maybe her face had lightened up more in line with her scars. She turned from Daud and headed back to her room. Daud worried that he had offended her. Why had he pushed her so hard? He thought the microwave was a compromise, but maybe she had seen it as a rebuke.

She came back from her room smiling. She was carrying a small box wrapped with red and green paper. She handed it to Daud. It was a bottle of cologne, something she'd seen for sale at the shop in the hotel.

"The important businessmen use it," she told him.

She said they shouldn't eat, because church was tonight. He didn't have to come with her. But Daud said he wanted to.

"Maybe we can have a little popcorn," she said. "Just to try it out."

Daud burned some of the popcorn, and the smell permeated the apartment. He'd do better next time. Daud ripped a hole in the bag and they ate together straight from it, taking turns thrusting their hands through the hole. Helen's long fingers slipped easily through the gap in Daud's hand. Butter lingered on the scars where his fingers had been.

On the bus to church, Daud asked Helen if they could stop at a drug store for dental floss. He had kernels of popcorn stuck between his teeth.

They walked together slowly to the church from the drugstore. Once the service started, Daud listened to the droning chant. Chanting was always in the language Geez, which was like Tigrinya only much older. Dawit understood only a few words, and he let it wash over him, the language seeming to change to Saho and Arabic and Tigrinya and English and languages he did not even know existed but were being spoken by families at tables somewhere in the world. David enjoyed rubbing his tongue against the pieces of popcorn sticking out of his front teeth. He liked the smell of cologne on him. He'd never thought of wearing any before, and had really been hoping Helen would get him an electric blanket instead, but now that he had it on, he imagined being the kind of person who would wear cologne from then on. The cologne mixed with the smell of incense and the faint but unmistakable hint of burnt popcorn that clung to them both.

Kian and Maggie

Desperate to get her son off his tablet, Maggie finally resorted to spanking, something it was her professional duty Monday through Friday to tell parents never to do. She shouted at him to get outside as loud as she thought she could get away with, considering the thin walls of the townhouse. It was a nice day. Not just a nice day, an unseasonably nice day, maybe the last one of the fall and that meant the last of the whole year. Who knew how long it would be before a day like this came again? They lived next to a park, for crying out loud, and they hardly ever used it.

Whatever the research she cited to her workshop parents said, Kian responded to spanking. He ignored polite requests, especially when they involved putting down his tablet. He didn't give a shit about a merit system involving stickers on a chart. He was sullen when told firmly to follow an order. He was downright rude, full of a vocabulary Maggie was sure she had not been aware of at age six, when given ultimatums. But when faced with the raw threat of physical harm, he could be made to resemble what she believed kids his age should act like for a few hours.

The widows' support group she attended on Friday nights (more for an hour of free day care than for the actual support it provided) would have been shocked to know she occasionally dabbled in corporal punishment.

She ran a wet cloth over his face to erase the crying lines, forced him through getting pants on, and tied his shoes—he had always worn shoes with Velcro straps and was still getting used to tying the loops. When she finished the double knots for him, at last they emerged outside, ready to get some kind of use out of this day and the park. For a few hours, she would be free of the guilt of being one of those mothers who used YouTube to babysit her child. Most of all, she would put off that creeping feeling of Sunday dissolving around her into another week of before-school drop-off meltdowns from Kian, and then work… no, that subject was banished for now.

As if to attack every good intention she had that day, they had barely crossed through the gap in the forsythia bushes separating the townhouses from the park when she heard the tortured notes of "Turkey in the Straw" pushed through a barely functioning loudspeaker. Maggie never bought Kian anything from the ice cream truck, but all the kids at the apartments they used to live at had made it their regular afternoon snack. It would have broken her father's heart for Maggie to do something as prodigal as buy from an ice cream truck. So she did for Kian what her dad had done for her: she explained the mark-ups the truck charged, how for the price of one Cookies 'n Cream bar, they could go to the grocery store and buy a whole box of popsicles. She allowed him to have a popsicle from the freezer every time the truck came by.

But as they were moving out of the apartments in June at the end of the school year, the freezer in the apartment was empty when the truck showed up. She had already shut off the Wi-Fi, and Kian was bored. Maggie, wanting to celebrate the end of kindergarten and their escape from the apartments, had walked with Kian to the truck.

"What do you want? They have cherry bombs…"

"That's it, Mom! I want a cherry bomb!"

"You sure you don't want something else? They have a lot of other things. There's…"

"No, I want a cherry bomb!"

It had ended up more on his face and hands than in his mouth, but he talked about it the rest of the day. Mom, Mom, Mom. I know it's more expensive than the store. But Mom, Mom, Mom. It's so good. Mom, Mom, Mom. Can we do that again sometime? If I don't bother you? Or if I try a new food? Or if I go outside and play?

She hadn't let him buy anything from the truck since they had moved into the townhouses, but he still ran outside when the truck came by. The first time, he had yelled to the driver to slow down, then come inside to ask Maggie for money. She had been forced to go outside and explain to the driver that her son had called to him without permission. After that, he continued to sprint outside when the truck went by, "just to see." But in August, he had taken money from her purse and snuck out to buy a cherry bomb without telling her. He left evidence all over his face, and also forgot to bring back the change he had set down to eat his treat, making it a twenty-dollar cherry bomb. She had spanked him so hard for that her own hand went numb, but he never went outside for the truck again.

Her phone chirped at her. Her dad texting again. Was she enjoying the new place? How was Kian doing at the new school? Was he still crying every time she dropped him off? She let go of Kian's hand to look at her phone, and Kian began to run toward the parking lot and the truck.

"Kian!" she rasped at him. He stopped and turned around, head down, seeming to remember his past with ice cream trucks.

"Why do we have to be at the stupid park today?"

"Because we're not going to become one of those families that sits inside and watches videos all day when it's nice out. Halloween's in a week. It may not be this nice again until April. We have to take advantage of it."

He sulked off toward the swings. There was one swing for big kids and one for babies. The swing was the only thing he liked at the park. His hair was garishly red, and it played off the crimson of the autumn leaves in the woods in the distance. The sun lit him up, and he glowed against the emerald green of the grass, the brown of the mulch beneath the swings. Maggie thought of the picture of her and Tim kneeling in front of a bale of hay, Kian balanced on Tim's knee between them. It was at a corn maze three years ago. It seemed like just another day with just another enriching experience for their son, not the last outing they would spend as a family.

Maggie's shadow on the grass was as thin as a sapling twig. Her phone twittered its second reminder that her dad had sent messages.

She pushed Kian on the swing. She felt like a first-grader should know how to push himself, but his playground at school didn't have swings because they were too dangerous, so maybe it wasn't his fault. She pushed him with one hand, only looking at him sideways to know when he had bobbed back up. She tried to push down thoughts of work the next day with each thrust, but they kept surging into her consciousness. Would the morning meeting go over an hour? If so, would she be able to wait that long to go to the bathroom if she drank coffee before? Would Jeff bring in donuts, and would he criticize her for not eating any? Would her boss Janice ask again when she would be starting grad school? Would Janice criticize her for writing the weekly memo in the new style, even though she had been the one to demand Maggie start using it? Would Maggie forget whether it was "its" or "it's"? Would someone mistake her for a secretary when her title said "coordinator of social services"? Would there be more talk of budget cuts, and the question of why they had a coordinator at all, especially one without a master's degree?

It was too early on a Sunday to be stressing about the week. It was enough they controlled her all week long. She couldn't give them her Sunday, too. If she did, where would it end? Would she no longer be able to enjoy Saturday mornings with Kian where they both stayed in her bed and watched his silly videos, then made pancakes at eleven? No, she had two days off, and she couldn't afford to keep giving most of one of them back. She took a picture of Kian flying away from her with her phone. He turned around at the sound and said he was bored and wanted to go home.

"Let's go walk the path and do the obstacles," she recommended.

"No, I hate that."

"Come on, you could use the exercise."

He hunched over and let the swing slowly run out of momentum. His feet scraped the ground beneath him coming and going. A girl in braids who had just arrived looked hopefully at them, waiting her turn.

"Come on, let's go walk the trail. If you do all the obstacles, you can have ice cream when we get home."

Kian slumped off the swing and the girl came running to take it. Maggie took his hand and they got on the footpath that ran into the woods. She talked about the path at the park she used to go to as a girl, and how that had started her running. She talked about how she ran cross-country in high school and then even in college, even though you had to be very good to be allowed to run for a college team. Kian said he thought Serebii was the fastest Pokémon.

The first obstacle was a balance beam. You were supposed to hop over it back and forth. Beginner's score was three times, expert was ten. Maggie hopped it ten times. Kian hopped it once.

"I did it."

"You have to do it the number of times the sign says."

"No, you didn't say that. You said if I did all the obstacles, I could have ice cream. You didn't say how many times I had to do them."

"Well, I'm saying it now. You have to do them the number of times on the sign."

"That's not fair. Anyway, the sign says three times."

"Not that one. The other number."

Kian stepped over the see-saw. Then he stepped back. Maggie grabbed his arm hard and stuck her nails into his biceps.

"Do it right or so help me, I will spank you right here on this path."

Kian sighed and rolled his eyes, but hopped back and forth with some agility ten times.

They walked the entire path, stopping for obstacles. Maggie took pictures when Kian was sliding across on the parallel bars. When she had enough pictures to prove she had orchestrated a happy family day out at the park, she would send them to her dad.

At the end of the mile-long loop, the park was much fuller than before. Families were done with church and enjoying the day outside. The parking lot was full of circling vans. A group of what looked like eight-year-olds was playing a baseball game. They had uniforms, and the coaches were instructing them with serious words like "Keep your shoulder back, Cody," and "We need to be backing up, middle infield!" The boys all responded quickly and compliantly. Mothers tended a cooler full of Gatorade. Maggie was astounded that the teams were playing so late in the fall. Travel teams were so competitive, they played until the weather made it impossible, ensuring kids—and their parents—stayed busy almost year-round.

She asked Kian to sit with her on top of a small hillock along the third base line and watch the game. Kian sat, then lay down and looked at the sky, flailing his arms around and humming a song he had invented.

She had forced Kian to play tee ball in the spring and regretted every minute of it. Kian complained before every game about having to go. He sulked in the field. If a ball was hit to him, he either didn't notice or jumped out of the way. Maggie ended up having to get in Kian's face before every game, threatening to spank him as hard as she could if he didn't at least try.

A cheer went up from the parents as the bat plinked against the ball. The boys on the field were so earnest. Maggie's sister had a son like that, and about that age. Daniel was good at sports and good in school, even though his father was a drunk who screamed all the time. They spanked Daniel. And look what he was like. Maybe that's what Maggie needed. Not to use force as a last resort for which she was more than half sorry, but to use it often, unapologetically, thereby maintaining total control.

Kian suddenly sat up and waved. Maggie looked in the direction he was looking; there were fifty kids running every which way in the jungle gym area, with its reassuring super-soft spongy matting. But nobody was waving back at Kian. He shot off toward the crowd, leaving Maggie struggling to get up and follow him.

Maggie walked. She didn't want to be a mother who had to be within five feet of her child wherever he went. She watched

Kian tap a little elvish looking boy on the shoulder. The boy's hair was gelled into a point in the front. From twenty yards away, she could see the boy's long eyelashes flutter open when he recognized her son. They embraced and soon had one another in headlocks. Kian yelled a word she didn't recognize, then the boy yelled it, too, and they were off chasing one another.

They roamed all over the circle of rubberized padding, zipping underneath slides and monkey bars, playing a game whose inscrutable rules they both seemed comfortable with. Mothers scooted closer to their wobbling toddlers, eyeing Kian and his friend warily. Maggie had received three notes from school that year about Kian not seeming to socialize well. She blamed the move from Piney Ridge—the assigned school when they'd lived at the apartments—to the new school at Hammond. He'd done better in his year of kindergarten at the old school. He now refused to participate in art, gym, or music, and his handwriting had become utterly unintelligible, even to Maggie. So who was this new boy? She assumed he was from Hammond, which was just on the north side of the park.

The boys were playing happily and Maggie didn't want to intervene, although many of the mothers and one father wearing khakis and sandals seemed to be looking around for an authority figure to keep the boys from running so dangerously close to their little ones. A man with short hair and broad shoulders came down from the railing surrounding the circular pit and said something to the boy Kian was playing with. Both boys followed him outside the ring and relocated to an area adjacent to the tennis courts.

She assumed the man was the boy's father; he glanced at the boys now and again while reading a book, something about the Civil War. He was the only person at the park with a book instead of a phone. She wondered how he could manage to forget about wherever he would have to go the next day and think about something that had happened so long ago. He seemed happy. He had early wrinkle lines and seemed several years older than Maggie, but the lines seemed to suggest laughter. She felt she might resent him for this. What right did anyone have to be reading a book on a Sunday, not thinking at all about what might happen at work that week?

She thought of her failed attempts to overcome anxiety about work with music. If she just listened to Beethoven in the car on the way in, and kept that music in her head at work, nothing would touch her. How could office lackeys with their banal concerns touch someone with something as transcendent as Beethoven to think of? But the office radio played pop, and Beethoven was gone from her head before lunch.

The short hair and broad shoulders walked towards her, smiling, a finger wedged into the page in the book to keep his spot. The other hand was extending itself toward her, and the mouth, separated by too large a space from the other features on the face, was talking. I'm Joshua's father. We live over on the other side of the woods. (The single-family homes, Maggie thought.) Joshua and Kian are friends from before-care at school. Joshua talks about Kian a lot. The kid who knows all about Pokémon because he watches videos on YouTube about them.

Maggie took the hand and wagged hers with it. She stared

stupidly at the face and said a name. Was he criticizing her for letting Kian watch videos too often? In the parenting class she taught to foster parents, the guidebook said to avoid power struggles. But avoiding power struggles meant letting him get what he wanted. If she didn't, he struggled. Maggie bet Joshua's dad avoided power struggles by winning the battles decisively right away. Shock and awe. That was the kind of parenting that got kids on travel baseball teams and winning Math Olympics.

"If I could get him to be as excited about math as he is about those videos," she said.

Joshua's father said his name, but Maggie could only think of him as "Joshua's dad." He said what he did, but it only sounded like something that made a lot of money and didn't have to worry about being squeezed out if his office was thought too small to keep his position. His wife was a doctor who delivered perfect babies into the world. They had two other children and one more coming. Kian and Joshua continued their shouting, grabbing, chasing, and jumping on one another. Kian was sweating, and had thrown his light jacket on top of a bush.

Maggie kept wishing she'd been a teacher and a cross-country coach. She wondered if she stopped running all the time, would her breasts grow enough to find a man who lived in the single-family houses so she could quit her job, focus on Kian? Or, if she got hit by a bus, would Joshua's father adopt Kian to live in a house full of happy kids with parents who didn't worry about Monday when it was still Sunday? She was wondering so many things, she didn't notice when the ice cream truck came back to the parking lot, even though its pinched, shrill theme song was somehow even louder than before. Maybe it was all the ads for Halloween horror movies, but it seemed macabre to her, a children's song warped and twisted on an endless loop. Joshua came running to his father, who handed him a few dollars from his wallet.

Kian, his face sporting a new freckle or two from the time in the sun, turning him red on red with red on top, looked to Maggie with absolute belief in the reasonableness of what he was about to ask.

"Mom. You said if I did all the obstacles—-all the numbers on the signs on all the obstacles—I could have ice cream. Can I just get something from the ice cream truck with Joshua instead?"

It was a reasonable request, reasonably advocated for. If Joshua's father hadn't made a comment before about the videos Kian watched, she'd have agreed to it readily. He'd been better than usual today, almost like a normal kid. Joshua's dad was right next to them, back to reading his book, but probably listening. She couldn't reward him with something extra, something outside the original agreement, just for doing what she had told him to do.

"We'll have ice cream when we get home. That was the deal."

"But a cherry bomb is just ice cream. Why can't I have that?"

"Because I said we'd have ice cream when we got home."

"But that's stupid! I don't want stupid crap generic ice cream when we get home. I want a cherry bomb with Joshua!"

Maggie felt a surge of opposing, powerful urges at once. On the one hand, Joshua was the first kid who resembled a friend

Kian had ever had. On the other hand, a kid who talked like Kian just had would lose any friend from the single-family homes. Maggie guessed Joshua's dad was already judging her, passing a verdict that his son would never play with a townie (yes, that's what he probably called those who lived in the townhouses on the other side of the park) with a mouth like that.

For Kian's own good, she had to stop his mouth. She had to stop him from letting the world see in public what she let him be at home. She grabbed his arm hard, digging her nails into his bare arms. She saw his face twist, felt him go limp trying to break the grip, but she held on tight and ground into his flesh.

Directly into his ear, she whispered harshly, "If you ever talk to me that way in public again, I will *end* you."

He began to cry, a little at first, then, without any reservation. Maggie knew this act from tee ball. Once he started to cry a little in front of everyone, his crying would switch suddenly from sad to angry. His words came in bursts. *Not fair. Why can't I just have something from the truck?That's all I asked for. Why do you have to hurt my arm? Why do you have to break my arm?* And he clutched his bent appendage, now showing four crescent-shaped welts in it. Maggie looked around. Nobody seemed to be watching. Joshua's father was immersed in his reading, maybe a little too conspicuously unconcerned. But she felt that when she wasn't watching, a dozen hands were reaching for their phones to call child services. She had to act like she had it under control.

"Kian, we don't talk disrespectfully to one another. I'm sorry I hurt your arm when I was trying to keep you from running away while I was talking to you. But I'm not going to change my mind about the ice cream truck, especially not for someone who calls me stupid."

Kian started to object that he hadn't called her stupid, only the decision to deny him a cherry bomb and the replacement of store brand fudge ripple ice cream in the freezer at home, but Maggie took a step towards him, and he flinched and retreated to the spot where he and Joshua had been playing. The sun came out from behind a cloud and the whole park was lit in the one perfect autumnal moment that comes every year. The trees in the woods shook in the breeze and their million leaves blended into a million new tints that existed only for that moment in history. The golden cattails of the swamp by the pond waved goodbye to all the beauty passing. Her son with his hair seemed to be the center of all that color. Her co-workers, looking at pictures of him on her desk, called it all the usual things people call red hair: ginger, fire-red, apple red, carrot-orange. It reminded Maggie of nothing so much as the bowling ball her father had bought her when she was not much older than Kian. She was never very good at bowling, but took great pride in the ball because it came from her dad.

All that color, loud as the speaker on the ice cream truck, and all of it just a cheat, a lie. It promised you things that weren't coming. She had once thought she would run marathons for a living. Ha! How retarded—she let herself think of it with a word she'd have smacked her son for using. Late October days weren't supposed to be this pleasant. By the middle of the week, she'd be clutching to the collar on her coat while she ran from the car to the office. Nothing was free. You pushed yourself through five terrible mornings just to get to one morning of pancakes and videos. But once you were there, you felt the full weight of how bad it had been getting to that one short moment of happiness, how much you didn't want to go out there and do it again. Better not to let yourself enjoy anything.

She had enjoyed being married to Tim, who was on the men's cross-country team in college. Before Kian, they picked 10Ks to run together and planned to eventually run one in all fifty states. When Kian came along, their plans ended after thirteen states, the same number as the original colonies. She'd tried not to give up, and had kept pushing Tim to keep training. She would run with Kian in the jogging stroller and log her miles on the refrigerator to push Tim to log his own. Tim got home late from work one night and it was already dark because Daylight Saving Time had just ended. He went running and got hit by a car.

Life had only been a long sprint for Tim, instead of the marathon it was turning into for Maggie. Maybe he was the smart one. One minute they had been winning medals, and the next they were struggling to keep up with jobs they hated to feed a son they barely understood. The other night, Maggie had awoken from a dream in which Kian was being crucified. She saw actual nails go through his hands and feet.

Her own childhood had seemed happy to her, with her sister and father and mother and everyone looking forward to the three weeks in Ontario every summer as the highlight of the year. Her mother let her heat water for hot chocolate in her Easy Bake oven. Then her mother was sick—just sick, nothing to worry about. But a few days later, she was dead, and Maggie couldn't remember what the last thing she said to her was. It hadn't seemed important when it happened. Her father raised the two kids himself, and Maggie couldn't believe how easy he made it seem. She was failing to raise one on her own.

Kian waited while Joshua neatly and evenly ate a Snickers Ice Cream Bar down to the end of the stick. They continued their game, but it seemed to have lost some of its energy. They replaced actual battles with notional ones, and Joshua allowed Kian to simply decide, using an esoteric calculus of his own devising, who emerged from each phase of combat with the edge. After thirty minutes, the air finally started to feel cool. Joshua's dad stuck a leaf in his book and tossed Joshua's sweatshirt over his shoulder. The short hair and broad shoulders were offering good-byes through the mouth that stood alone. Kian and Joshua looked at one another, some secret plot between the two now reaching its moment to launch.

"Mom, can Joshua come over?" Kian asked.

Maggie halted, unsure what to answer. She would be happy to let Kian do anything that normal kids did, but was afraid of saying yes. If she did, she thought Joshua's dad might invent reasons why his son should not visit the home of a townie. But he didn't even let Maggie respond.

"We don't have time today, bud," he said. "But maybe next weekend we can." He turned to Maggie. His raised eyebrows and crinkled skin that undulated up his bare forehead seemed to indicate sincerity. "Why don't I give you my cell number?"

Maggie used it as a chance to confirm the father's name (Jeff).

She thanked Joshua for playing with Kian. As they turned to go, Maggie let her happiness get the best of her.

"Hey, Kian," she said, loud enough for Jeff to hear. "I see the truck is still over there. How about we go get that cherry bomb now?"

The driver was almost asleep when they came to the window. It took him a minute to find a cherry bomb, but he finally produced one after bending over deep into one of the freezers. It was freezer burnt, but Kian attacked it with abandon. Maggie went down by the tennis courts to retrieve his jacket from the bush and realized she was still holding her phone in her hand from when she had put Jeff's number into it. She took a minute to send the pictures of the day to her dad. Kian swinging, without Maggie in the picture so it looked like he was doing it on his own. Kian walking across a balance beam in front of wine-tinged blackgum trees. Kian holding on to the pullup bar, looking like he was about to do a pull-up, although in reality he hadn't been able to do one.

The response from her dad was immediate.

Looks like a perfect day.

Maggie sniffed out a tiny laugh. Looks like it, yeah.

The cherry bomb was now one with Kian's face. It was late afternoon and getting cooler. Kian was shivering while eating his treat. She herded him back in the direction of the town houses. She hadn't gone to the store to replace the stock of chips, juice, and children's protein bars that were the only things he'd eat in his lunch. She hadn't washed their clothes for Monday. She hoped his Halloween costume she'd ordered late would come on time. Goodness, Halloween. That must mean soon they'd be setting the clocks back an hour. If they came this time next week, it might be dark already. Then Thanksgiving and Christmas, when it would get darker and darker still, followed by however many repetitions of all of this it took to raise him to be whatever he was going to be.

Dawn Doesn't Disappoint

The nice thing about Dawn is she doesn't expect anything. Of you, of her job, of the world. Her thighs, which, if I may play the poet for a moment, could be a sort of synecdoche for all of her—or is it metonymy? I can never remember—take whatever form they happen to be smashed into when she shifts in her chair at her computer. I used to watch them beneath her miniskirt, like two beige anacondas whose lunch was going down and back up repeatedly. She had a different miniskirt for every day of the week, each a primary color and all of them too short for a dumpy girl like her to pull off. Since she wasn't a threat to the better looking women in the office, like Amy, who always wore dark hose with her skirts, or Liz, who wore jeans because she was just a temp but still looked great in them, none of them snickered about Dawn behind her or in front of her. Because she was overweight, I think others naturally assumed she was good-natured. After about six months of sneaking off for sex with her, I can confirm that she isn't bad-natured, anyhow.

She was a very junior product analyst, which meant she was the first person to see all the new whiz-bang ideas entrepreneurs wanted to sell to our stores so we could sell them to others. It was her job to triage the slew of ideas coming in and to pass on the ideas with promise to a senior product analyst like me. Most products people dream up are bad, so it's easy to just get in the rut of saying no to everything. A front-line analyst needs to take breaks to clear her head of the last ten bad ideas so if a good one comes in, she can recognize it.

I remember I learned the word "triage" from the show M*A*S*H. She'd never seen it, of course.

I wouldn't have guessed I'd be fooling around with her when she first showed up, even though it had been so long since Ella left, I was starting to wonder if my equipment still worked. Nights when I didn't have the boys, I'd sometimes try Internet porn, but I think I've finally seen all the porn there is to see on the Internet. I'd been lifting weights to try to get my testosterone back up, but then I tore my rotator cuff. It was my first week of suffering through rehab when Dawn came to the office.

At first, I thought she had the kind of face where you'd say she was pretty if it wasn't for—you know. But the longer I watched her staring into her monitor, straight cheeks flanking a flat mouth with a bulbous nose in the middle, the more I thought she was a girl you'd just call plain if it weren't that being fat made you think her face wasn't the problem.

Then again, youth looks good on everybody.

I felt bad when I first found myself looking down at her legs or up at her breasts—on most days, barely more tucked in than her thighs were—as she stood next to me while I explained how to make use of the market predictions tools. She was a lot older than my kids, but still young enough that I could have biologically pulled off the feat of having a daughter her age if I'd been able to find a girl willing to ruin her future with me when I was seventeen. One Friday, though, as we were all pulled in a circle shooting the shit about the weekend to come, her skirt slipped an extra inch or two up toward her hips, and I saw a birthmark covering most of the meaty part of her quadriceps. When Bob and Anne—who were, I'd long thought, flirting their way dangerously close to a couple of divorces with their respective spouses themselves—got up to grab some donuts, I used it as a conversation piece.

"It looks like the Millennium Falcon," I said, allowing myself a long and uninterrupted look at her drumstick of an appendage.

"Everyone else always says it looks like West Virginia," she said.

It was two points sticking out of a dark brown blob. If I'd been looking at it upside down, which I soon would do, it might have even looked like a devil with horns. I explained to her why the Millennium Falcon was so important to men my age, how it had been the stuff of our dreams when we were young. As I told her about Han Solo, whom she had never heard of, I traced my finger around the outline of her birthmark. My finger left a red trail across her skin, which sank beneath the weight as I skimmed over her leg. It felt like gravy in a Ziploc bag. I liked that the color changed.

I wish I could say that dating a younger woman made me younger and temporarily better, but let's be honest, we weren't really dating. She didn't make any demands on me, either, like I'd worried a younger woman might. I didn't have to lose ten pounds or read Sylvia Plath or go clubbing with her. She was as pliant as her quadriceps, which took whatever form they fell into by chance, depending on the shape of their container. Or lack of a container.

Not so my physical therapist, who pushed me and punished me and humiliated me three times a week in exchange for my twenty-dollar co-pay. She was as thin as the stretch cords she made me labor with, and just as strong. The small patches of lingering acne from her teen years did nothing to diminish how attractive she was. They only made it more obvious how lucky a man would be to have her, because if she could look that good with a few red splotches on her nose, imagine what she'd be like when she finally grew out of it. It was almost a shame that her face would be as clear as Dawn's one day.

She was getting married soon. All the talk from the other therapists was about the upcoming wedding. There was envy in their voices. The groom was a med student.

A man my age who drove a much nicer car than I do was always on the table next to me at therapy. He'd shattered his knee hang gliding in the Andes. He plied her endlessly with questions she gave one-word answers to. I was afraid to say anything to her, even if I didn't understand what exercise I was supposed to do. I sweated and winced beneath the effort of my side-lying external rotations. I didn't want to let her down.

She told me at one point that I was too old to lift heavy weights. It wasn't my muscles, it was my joints. They were drying out, she said. She suggested I take yoga. I ventured the only sarcastic comment I ever made to her, that I didn't want to be the only man in the class.

"Men don't take yoga because they're stubborn," she said. "Seems like the first person to join the class would have a competitive advantage, dude-to-chick ratio-wise."

It turned out there were five men in the yoga class I tried. Two were college football players willing to give anything a shot. Three were gay. I stayed and put up a good fight on my mat in the back of class until my two months of therapy were up. I was with Dawn. I was already in good enough shape for that.

It's not that I never felt guilty about taking advantage of her. Twice, I took her out on real dates on nights when I didn't have the boys. She thanked me for her dinners, her movie, her ticket to an artsy and therefore unattended play, but she didn't seem terribly excited to have gone. I would have brought her back to my place, where we could have had proper sex in a bed instead of against the wall of the supply closet, but she asked me to drop her off at home. She didn't invite me in.

To tell the truth, I don't know if I could even have had sex with her any other way than standing up behind her in the supply closet.

She was terrible at picking products that would sell. I shot down nine of ten ideas she brought to me. The numbers were all off. I didn't get it. She wasn't dumb. I'd heard her hold her own in conversations about Supreme Court decisions, French art, Nineteenth Century Latin American revolutions, and writing in JavaScript. But when it came to picking a product, she'd ignore all the research and try to sell me on a t-shirt that was also a bra, a frame for making igloos out of snow, a trick football tee that would sling a football forward after you tapped it, making it look like you just kicked a fifty-yard field goal on your own, reversible work boots that you could wear on either foot so you didn't wear grooves in the soles so fast, a pregnancy test with a long handle so the partner could hold the test under the urine stream to be part of the excitement, or a thumb drive with retractable wings so it could double as a glider. She was like an old-school baseball scout who throws away all the stats and numbers and goes with his gut, only for her everything her gut was telling her was shit.

I couldn't blame her: she didn't seem to want anything for herself, so how could she know what anyone else might want? I was starting to think the nicest thing I could do for her would be to fire her so she could find something more suited to her. I tried to imagine what kinds of positions there were for people willing to completely take their cues from others. Prostitute. Not for her without some major changes. Nun. Same thing. Maybe a politician?

Problem was, of course, that I couldn't fire her. I didn't think she'd be the kind to file a sexual harassment suit, but I felt guilty as hell for fucking someone eighteen years younger than me, and in this economy, jobs are hard to come by for young people. I thought if I just kept telling her every idea she had was a bad one, she'd get the hint that this field wasn't for her. But every day was a new skirt: red like a lifeguard's first-aid kit; blue like an autism awareness light bulb; yellow like a wet-floor sign. If nobody told her to stop, she'd keep coming in to work as a junior product analyst until the rapture.

She told me one day while I was zipping back up that this was the seventy-seventh time we'd done it. "Double lucky," she said. She was double lucky to have ended up with me. I knew I needed to get her out of there. But she was so satisfied with where she was. The only way to make her unsatisfied enough to leave was to make her want something more.

One of the other branches had a bright young app consultant with protruding crooked teeth, a short neck and a loud voice. Ian was going places, if only he could avoid the hatred of the people who might decide to pay him enough to keep him. He wouldn't make enough money to overcome his looks, at least not while working with us. But he was probably just about right for Dawn. I figured if I got the two of them together, they'd find their level, the way water wants to spill into a void. I asked for Ian to come to my team, saying I needed someone smart to make up for having Dawn. My division manager Kyle, who is younger than me and I think knew I was fucking Dawn, looked at me side-eyed but approved the request. Ian's old manager couldn't stand to listen to him anymore, and didn't put up a fight.

But the dumb kid wouldn't take the bait. I sat him where he'd be right in Dawn's line of sight. I asked her to wear her shortest skirt the first day he was in the office. I held a team meeting and asked them to introduce themselves to each other. I dragged out a part of it so she and he could exchange long answers on where they grew up, what their hobbies were, where they saw themselves in five years. They were both from random farm towns: Michigan for her and Southern Virginia for him. She couldn't name a hobby but he named enough for both of them, all of them having to do with making weapons by hand that he sold at Renaissance fairs. In five years, they both said they hoped to be married. That was a surprise coming from her, but a happy one, if only he took the hint.

But that stupid son of a bitch kept trying to flirt with Amy, even though she obviously wasn't interested and everyone knew she had a boyfriend who would take her away from the office just as soon as he made enough money to knock her up. Ian actually brought her in a medieval queen's gown made of green velvet and about a hundred loops and buttons.

"I traded one of my best broadswords to get this," he said, as she stood, dumbfounded, not stretching out her hands to take it from him. "Now you'll have something to wear if you ever go to a Renaissance festival and you want to go in costume." Amy ran out of the room, and I wasn't sure if she was laughing or crying. Ian laid the dress over the top of Amy's cubicle. Amy left it lying on top of the trash can that night.

That night, I called Dawn at home. She was eating toasted cheese and chicken noodle soup. I told her people always ate toasted cheese with tomato soup; she said she'd never heard of such a thing.

"Did you mean what you said today? About wanting to be married in five years?"

"Sure I did," she said.

"You know that with me, there's not much chance of that, right?"

"I guess so."

I rubbed my shoulder on the scar. I should have been doing

my rehab exercises. I should have been walking. I should have been eating better. I should have been reading a book. "I mean it. Ella got a lot out of me in the divorce. I felt guilty, so I didn't fight her. My child support alone is like one-fourth of my paycheck. I can't afford to be starting over. I lost in life. I don't want to start the game over again."

"I know." Something clinked on her side of the phone.

"Can't you eat your soup without banging your spoon on the bowl?"

"I'm eating ice cream now."

"Well, I wish you'd stop."

"I can eat quieter."

"No, I mean stop eating ice cream. Stop eating so much in general. You eat too much. You need to lose weight."

"No problem. You're right, she said." I heard her bowl hit the sink and water running into it.

I decided to press my luck that night with women by calling Ella. She was fighting with the boys about going to bed. Danny was a year older than Marcus, but they woke up at the same time to be dropped off early at school, so she wanted them to go to bed at the same time. Danny considered this an affront to his status as first-born. When they slept at my house, one stayed in my bed and the other on the couch. I had to put them to bed one at a time, so I did Marcus first and Danny ten minutes later. This was enough that he felt honored.

"It's your fault he demands special treatment," Ella complained. "He says you let him stay up later."

"By like ten minutes."

"It's enough to cause major headaches for me here...*Now,* I said!"

I knew I didn't have much time. "Look, Ella, I know the divorce agreement says no women around the kids. But I've been seeing someone for a couple of months now, and..."

"Is it serious?"

"Getting there," I said. "I'm not saying right now, but in a couple of weeks, maybe."

"We'll see. Does she know how much you've underperformed in life? That you scored a 177 on your LSAT and chose not to go to law school because you 'can't stand lawyers?' That you now work selling junk for Bargain Barn so you don't have to be challenged?"

"She works for me."

Ella laughed and laughed at that one. She hung up the phone still laughing.

Dawn started losing weight. I noticed within a week. At first, it had a negative effect on her appearance. She was still fat, but not so fat you forgave her the way she looked. Whatever softening of her face all those pounds had been granting her was gone, leaving her with just bones and angles. It was like she was carrying around two knives on the sides of her face, warning everyone to back off and give her space. Eventually, though, enough of her shrank that it all started to fit together nicely. The last few weeks of it was like watching big piles of dirty snow in the parking lot you'd been avoiding all winter melt until those few clear bits of asphalt that had been peeking through became one big, off-white slab shining in the sun.

Ian began to show her some attention, and I think maybe Shaun from budget did, too, but she wouldn't give them the time of day. She still wanted to sneak off with me to the supply room. All that weight she'd lost made it like doing it with a whole new person, so it was fun for me, I have to admit, but I'm kind of a self-contradiction when it comes to women. I like a woman who'll push me a little bit, even though I fight it the whole time. Ella gave up on waiting for me to "try for more in life." Just because I told her I didn't want to hear it anymore! When she made partner only five years out of law school, she told me it was time for me to move out. I expected that she would soon replace me with another high-powered lawyer from the firm, but she's stayed single all this time. I would know: Marcus can't keep a secret about anything.

Dawn isn't the type to push you. As she kept losing weight, I slid further into middle-aged pastiness. My shoulder hurt all the time, and I had to prop my arm up with a stack of computer paper at my desk. Meanwhile, I was singing Ian's praises every day to Dawn. I gave more than half my work to him, and I wasn't shy about letting everyone hear how lost I'd be without him. She started to ask him for help with some of her projects; he'd explain to her how to use the applications our company had developed at great expense, but without any greater success than I'd had. He also tried putting his hand in the middle of her back and guiding her in front of his keyboard to try out the feature in the application he'd just explained, with far less success than I'd had just grabbing her thigh.

I was going to have to be cruel about it and let her go. Not just from me, but from the company. As long as she was around, the temptation to keep indulging in our afternoon trips to the closet would be too much for me. It was like having junk food in the house. Even skinny, Dawn was like a pack of pink Hostess Sno-balls. She'd sit there until you couldn't take it anymore, and then you'd rip the cover off and eat one. Since the second goes bad once the package is open, you'd just go ahead and eat that one, too, and then you'd feel like shit the rest of the day. Maybe this simile is too strained.

I decided to let her make her own decision about a product, and to invest a significant amount of company capital in it. I led her to believe that I was going to let her call the shots on this one, and that I'd be behind her even though I disagreed with it. I sent her an e-mail that said the same thing. I told Kyle that I'd had it trying to explain to her that her ideas were rotten, and that the only way for her to learn was to let her take a hit on a bad buy. When it went south, I promised him, she'd either quit or I'd fire her myself. There'd be enough of a paper trail to keep us from a lawsuit.

Before I fired her, though, I wanted to arrange one meeting at my apartment with Ella and her. I asked Dawn to wear something nice and hired someone to clean my apartment for me. I can do it, but I'm never critical enough of the work I do myself. I'm so used to the gray spots in the bottom of the tub, I forget they can actually be powered off if you put time and muscle into it. There's a freeway ramp from forty-one to eighty-one, and I had somehow gotten myself on it. I couldn't figure out how to do a U-turn myself. The only way I could see myself going one step at a time through the long chain of events to get back on track—get serious about rehab, get back in shape, restore self-esteem and sense of urgency, re-apply to law school, attend night school, quit my job, get Ella back—was to send up an emergency flare to Ella and ask her to make me do it. God help me, I'm one of those people who will do nothing if left to his own devices, but will do anything if only a tough enough coach is in my face yelling at me to do it.

The meeting was short, only thirty minutes or so. I'd invited Ella for cake and coffee, because I didn't think I could pull off dinner. Dawn and I sat as close together as I could arrange. I set up a blanket in the family room so the boys could eat on the floor and leave the adults a little space. I wanted Ella to realize how desirable I was to a younger woman. It was hard for Dawn and me to squeeze together: my kitchen table is a rectangle, and we both had to sit with one of the legs between our thighs. I tried to scoot next to her, but my left knee kept getting held up, and I wasn't very flexible, so it would only bend so much.

I asked Ella what she was up to at work. She was busy with defending one or another little guy who'd been trodden on by a stronger force: tenants whose landlords failed to fix water heaters, car buyers whose dealers were not honoring their warranties, employees wrongfully terminated, a woman who'd been electrocuted by a faulty wire in a subway station. I was a little anxious for her to skip past the wrongful termination suit with Dawn in the room, but I feigned interest.

"What would you say if I told you I'm thinking of re-taking the LSAT and applying to go to law school part time at night?" I asked her. I leaned awkwardly toward Dawn at this point, as if to indicate that Dawn was my inspiration for getting my shit together, that all I'd needed all along was someone young and kind to inspire me.

"You're taking the LSAT?" Ella asked me. Too direct.

I'm thinking about it. I mean, I just started looking stuff up online, but yes, I'm probably taking it."

"I'd say see how you do and then decide."

"I did well before."

"And so you'll probably do well again."

Dawn hadn't eaten any of her cake. I nudged her and told her to eat some. Because I was at such an awkward angle, I nearly pushed her out of her chair when I nudged her. She had to make a desperate grab for the table to keep from pitching over toward the floor.

"Eat something," I told her, pretending not to notice how close I'd come to knocking her down. I turned confidentially to Ella and lamented with a grimace about how Dawn never eats anything.

"Which law school were you thinking of attending?" Ella asked me, tilting her cup straight up and then straight horizontally to her mouth to sip it.

Because in that moment I couldn't think of a single name of a college near us that I was sure had a part-time law program, I said that I'd only just begun to think about it. Because I'd nearly knocked her off her chair and scolded her for not eating after I'd scolded her for eating too much, Dawn got angry with me. She yelled at me after Ella took the boys, after Ella said she liked Dawn and she could be around the boys whenever I had them. Dawn had worn a new dress that was soft-colored and went all the way down to her calves. Because I'd tried to fire her after she dumped me, and because, maybe, Ella had just put the idea in her head, she threatened to sue the company for sexual harassment. Because her stupid idea for a two hundred-dollar water balloon howitzer became the company's big seller and gave us a record-setting quarter, and because I'd been stupid enough to say it was all her idea, the company was quick to take Dawn's side and fire me.

Am I skipping too fast through all the important parts of the story? I can never tell which are the most important. Did I take a speed ramp from one part of the story straight to the end? It all happened too fast for me to recall exactly how it went down. I remember Ian, who got promoted in my wake, telling me not to beat myself up over not foreseeing the success of Dawn's product. He hadn't seen it coming, either. "All the data really tells us is that what people want doesn't make any sense," he said.

I teach yoga now, a year later. I started going right after I got fired, and just kept going and going. I spent six hours a day on my mat, not even moving it off the floor of the studio between one class and another.

The first classes I went to as a student, there were few other men. With so little competition, it became easy to strike up a conversation with some of the women there. Don Draper may have taken yoga up at the end of *Mad Men* as a form of enlightenment, wanting to break away from all that womanizing he'd done, but I tell you, just the simple demographics of the matter make it a good bet he'd have been back to it pretty quick. I'm with one of the women from my classes now. She's the third since Dawn. Yoga is teaching me flexibility. When I no longer fit into another person's life, I just bend around it, start somewhere else. That road from forty to eighty was a result of my own narrow mind. There are so many roads, so many paths! My shoulder feels great. I feel great.

I don't know what I was thinking trying to lift all those heavy weights.

American as Berbere

For Meb, and everyone I know like him.

When he was twelve, Tesfay came to the conclusion that all Habesha music had a drum beat that sounded like somebody had chucked two shoes into a laundromat dryer, and soon thereafter he developed a contempt for Ethiopian music—and perhaps Ethiopia in general—that stuck with him. There had been a few years, soon after he came to the United States at eight, a fugitive of famine and the Derg's policies he knew nothing about, when he would listen with admiration to the beat of the *kebero*, as the horns and *krar* and flute-like thing with the name he couldn't pronounce all worked around it, like revelers weaving their strands around a Maypole. But over time, it became harder for the Greater D.C. Tigrayan People's Cultural Center to find anyone who knew how to play the *krar*, so they settled for a competent drum player and a synthesizer. In this arrangement, Tesfay heard only the drum's repetitious "ba-bump, ba-bump" drubbing away at the same speed. It filled him with a sense of futility, that no matter how many times someone hit the drum, the cycle would just keep going around, until someone finally yelled "*d'rub!*" and the drummer sped up to reach the merciful death of the song.

When he first came to the U.S. in 1984, he was a minor celebrity, having appeared as one of the crying children in a rock music benefit for Africa video, his distended abdomen hanging from him like an empty *taff* sack. A philanthropic organization sponsored his mother, younger brother Tsegaye and his sisters Meheret and Azeb to come as refugees. Their three-bedroom apartment on the west side of Baltimore had been handed over to them with some fanfare, newspapers snapping pictures of him and one of the lesser-known stars from the chorus of the rock anthem to end poverty. A councilwoman had even handed his mother the key to the front door. After the cramped shanties they had shared with dozens of others at the refugee camps in Ethiopia's Tigray region and later Sudan, having an entire room to just himself and his brother gave him a nauseating sense of agoraphobia. He felt abandoned and had to keep looking across the room to Tsegaye while his younger brother made up stories to accompany the comic books they had been given but couldn't read. Tesfay's first winter in America, he believed his new country was cold because there weren't enough people in it to keep it warm. He came down with pneumonia that kept him out of school for weeks.

A year later, their grant ran out. His mother who, in one year of attending English classes twice a week had learned nothing but "hello" and "nice to meet you," took a job cleaning bathrooms in office buildings with another Habesha woman who had started her own business. She didn't earn enough to put food in the mouths of her children, let alone pay rent and utilities, so the family had to move in with Aunt Sophia in Silver Spring, near

D.C. There were no cameras that came to record the day the family moved out, one garbage bag per person.

Aunt Sophia was a legend in the D.C. Habesha community. She was the sister of Tesfay's late father, who had been killed (martyred, Tesfay would later learn to say) in the struggle against the Derg. Aunt Sophia, whose own husband had also gone out a martyr, made her money selling home mortgages to Habesha families who would not take a loan from anyone who couldn't tell them their interest rate in Tigrinya or Amharic. She must have made a lot of money that way, because she supported half the TPLA back in Ethiopia with what she sent them, as well as keeping afloat a large number of destitute souls in America. She had enough left over for a four-bedroom with a loft into which her sister-in-law's family could squeeze without too much trouble, although Tesfay and Tsegaye had to share a room with her only son, Robel.

When Tesfay entered the house for the first time, he noticed a trophy almost as high as the ceiling. It had four pillars on the bottom, then two more pillars on a second level, and finally a golden man on top holding a stick and twisting his torso with the stick in his hand. Tesfay thought it was made entirely of gold and believed his aunt must be the richest woman in the world.

He heard his cousin yell "Heads up!" and saw a blur out of his left eye before he felt a crushing blow blind that same eye. He vaguely remembered lying, face up, trying to focus on the stalactites of paint from the ceiling while his aunt screamed in English at her son.

Later, as he was lying on the couch, his cousin sat on the floor next to him, holding a Ziploc bag full of ice cubes on his eye for him. *He-Man* was playing on the television. Tsegaye had already taken Tesfay's bag to their new room. Robel kept apologizing to Tesfay, saying he thought Tesfay could catch a baseball. Robel loved baseball. That's what the enormous trophy was for. Robel laughed when Tesfay asked how much it was worth. It was just plastic with gold paint.

Aunt Sophia kept peeking in at them while Tesfay recovered. She scolded Robel several times, but eventually seemed won over by his vigilant care for Tesfay. She kissed him on the top of his head, called him "Robeley," and sent him to set the table for dinner. She and Tesfay's mother had made injerra and shiro with *berbere* pepper. Aunt Sophia praised Robel for knowing how to open the prayer with the correct Orthodox incantation.

Tesfay's mother insisted that both he and Tsegaye learn to play baseball. Tesfay wondered if his mother thought baseball was essentially the same as soccer, the only game she had ever heard of. Or maybe baseball was to be part of their education in becoming Americanized, and Robel, holder of the glittering trophy, was to be their mentor.

That spring, Tesfay went to school during the day, where he slowly learned to say he was *confused* rather than *confusing*, to hear the difference between *live* and *leave*, and to contract all sorts of things into shorter things that meant the same thing. He was in the same class as Robel, and sensed his cousin was the sort of student who did not often know the answers, but hid it through a sleight of hand that allowed him to change the conversation at the crucial moment. An ample supply of friends who knew the answers didn't hurt.

Once home from school, Tesfay, Tsegaye and Robel always went straight to the playground to play baseball. Robel was patient in trying to explain how to swing, throw or catch, but when he threw batting practice to Tesfay, Robel would not hold back, and fired one pitch after another as hard as he could past Tesfay, who could scarcely get the bat started before the ball was already past him. Sometimes, Robel hit Tesfay, and they would retreat to the couch in the living room and repeat the scene from Tesfay's first day in the house.

"You have to be careful with your cousin, Robeley," his mother would say in between calls to clients seeking loans. "He's not as good as you."

"I have to throw hard at him, *adey*. The kids in the league are going to throw hard at him."

"Just be careful, Robeley."

Tesfay played on the same team as his cousin. Robel hit third in the lineup, the spot reserved for the best hitter. Tesfay played two innings a game, the minimum each player was required to be in the lineup, always in right field. While Robel pitched and batted his team to most of the wins they managed that year, Tesfay did not manage once to even put the bat on the ball. He was terrified of the ball and hoped for nothing more than to survive his few trips to the plate.

He only ran the bases once. It was the last inning of a game his team was losing by one run, and one of the good hitters at the top of the order managed a double, but hurt himself sliding into second. Robel told his coach that Tesfay was fast, and would be a good pinch runner.

Tesfay was fast. He took a runner's stance at second base, like he had seen others do all season long, and waited while Robel stood in the batter's box. On the second pitch, Robel sent a screaming line drive into centerfield. Tesfay did not wait. He tore off toward third base and rounded third toward home. He was a little awkward as he took the turn, but he was more than fast enough to make up for it. He heard the cries from his bench and the parents of his teammates, and it spurred him on to run even faster. He crossed home plate and waited for the kids from his team to come running out to congratulate him. It took him some effort to realize that the center fielder had caught Robel's line drive and thrown Tesfay out at second base, where he had failed to tag up, for the last out of the game. He had been called out at second while he was halfway from third to home. The shouts from his team had been to go back to second. The other team had been laughing at him as he streaked for what he'd thought was the tying run.

Tesfay sat with his head down in the dugout and refused to line up to shake the other team's hands. He did not huddle with his team to hear the coach tell them to shake it off and get the next one, nor did he take a juice box and a bag of chips someone had brought for the after-game snack. He waited until his family was loaded up in the van, then dragged himself to the back seat, not looking at anyone from the dugout to the parking lot. As he sat, his arms crossed and his cap pulled down over his eyes, his mother continually turned around to congratulate him for his performance. He had run so fast, she said. She could not understand that running fast was not the whole point of the game.

Tesfay tried to hide in his room that evening, but Robel and Tsegaye were there. He tried the basement, but Robel followed him. For the first time, he began to feel that the house he was living in was too small. He eventually opted for the living room, where at least the television was a distraction for others, and he could rely on being ignored. But after *Family Ties* ended, Robel got up and changed the channel to the Orioles game.

"We need to watch so Tesfay knows the rules," he said.

While the family watched Cal Ripken, Jr. work a walk, Tesfay stood up from the couch, stepped deliberately to Robel's trophy, and tipped it over with no more effort than he would have used to turn on a light switch. The swinging man on the top of the trophy hit the floor, broke off and ricocheted toward the television, barely missing hitting the screen.

His sisters, aunt, mother and Robel turned to him, as if waiting for an explanation, some improbable excuse about how he had just been admiring it and not meant to smash it. Instead, Tesfay stood, his arms pushed straight down at his sides and ending in two fists balled up like burnt bread.

"You never told me the rules, Robel."

Aunt Sophia started after him first, but when his mother realized what was happening, she quickly jumped up and won the race to Tesfay, pummeling him on the ears with slaps and pulling him by the hair. Robel came to his aid, and tried to get his mother off him.

"It's okay, Aunt Feven. It's okay! He's right. I didn't tell him the rules."

But he couldn't speak any language Tesfay's mother could understand, and the only words of his language she knew meant nothing right now. She beat Tesfay until he forgot that he was angry, was only aware that she was hurting him. He tried to ask for mercy, but his throat was so sore from holding back his tears, he could get out nothing except a slight, croaking "*bejabi, adey*."

✦✦✦

Tesfay held his balance for ten seconds, twenty, thirty, his left hand holding his left foot aloft behind him. His knee formed an upside-down goose neck while he stretched his quadriceps. He was wearing the headphones his mother had bought him when she took over her boss's cleaning business. They were the best, and he could scarcely hear a thing outside of Brahms' violin concerto. He had loved Brahms since joining the orchestra in seventh grade, because of the way his teacher over pronounced the German: "Bwghaaahms." Tesfay had tried his best to reproduce it at home in front of Robel. Robel, instead of a violin, had a large drum set that he tinkered with sometimes. He tried to introduce Tesfay to Stevie Ray Vaughan, but Tesfay assumed that if Robel liked it, it was probably a bad influence. That was what Aunt Sophia called everything and everyone Robel liked then: a bad influence.

Tesfay never played baseball after that year when he broke Robel's trophy. Robel played through high school and was good, but not good enough to earn a look from any scouts. Some said he had been too lazy and relied too much on his talent. Others said he was distracted by tinkering around with music and smoking pot and the girls who had taught him how to groove to both.

So Tesfay became a violin-playing non-athlete, and had the social status to match. Robel once tried to convince some of the school's jocks not to pick on him by telling them that Tesfay had grown up during the famine in Ethiopia. When the school got a hold of a video from the library of him at six, naked with his stomach protruding beyond his infant penis, things took a dangerous turn. Phys Ed was the worst. Anytime he wasn't looking during volleyball or football, a ball somehow found its way to his head. Someone would then come running over to offer profuse apologies and explanations about how the ball had just gotten away from him. The only bright spot was that it was the last period of the day, and Tesfay was spared from showers with his tormentors.

Eventually, Tesfay offered his P.E. teacher a deal. If Tesfay ran the whole time during gym, he would not have to take part in any of the sports being played. Tesfay hoped that if he could turn himself into a moving target, he'd be harder to hit. His teacher never believed that Tesfay could keep moving for fifty-two minutes, so he took the bargain. Three months later, his gym teacher brought someone to meet Tesfay while he was running his laps.

"This is Coach Hoffman. He's the cross-country coach."

Tesfay stopped to say hello, but felt uncomfortable not running. "You mean you travel a lot?" he asked.

Soon, Tesfay had as many trophies in the living room as

Robel. Then he had more. His senior year, Coach Hoffman stopped Tesfay during a practice to introduce him to yet another new person. It was the largest man Tesfay had ever seen, both in height and width.

"This is Coach De Sapio, Tesfay," he said. "He's the track coach at University of Maryland."

Tesfay shook his hand. Coach De Sapio's eyes were hidden by small, round sunglasses perched on top of his puffy cheeks."

"We've been getting our asses kicked lately by schools with all the best Kenyan runners," the coach said. "We were hoping you could change that."

"Well, I'm from Ethiopia, not Kenya," Tesfay said.

"Well, I won't tell anyone. As long as you can run like a Kenyan."

Tesfay won his first ACC title two years later in the 10,000 meters. He won his second a year after that, a day before he found out Robel had been killed, shot in the head and the forearm. The police did not know who had shot him, but they figured he had been shot in the forearm when someone pointed at his head and he had instinctively put up his arm. Tesfay wondered if Robel had tried to catch the bullet like it was a line drive. When Tesfay wanted to withdraw from the nationals, his Aunt Sophia would not let him.

"If I can lose a husband and come to America and start a business, and your mother can lose a husband and come to America and run a business, you can lose a cousin and run around in circles a few times."

He relaxed his hold on his foot, and the final strains of the concerto faded away in his ears. Rather than start a new piece of music so close to the race, he removed his headphones and looked up into the stands. Usually, it was easy to find his mother and sister Azeb. Meheret, his other sister, was off at college herself, as was Tsegaye, although they had sent their love and best wishes. Today, it was impossible to find his family in the crowd, because they were surrounded by a sea of Habesha faces, already bursting at the seams to cheer for him, waving the green, yellow and red flag of Ethiopia. Some wore their traditional white clothing. The heads of a few women were covered by *netsella*. They erupted into cheers when Tesfay looked up at them, and the flags circled happily like the vultures he had once seen descend upon a dead calf in Tigray. Tesfay laughed and waved, but ended his wave with a slight swipe of the hand that hinted at rejection. He wondered if they understood he was trying to qualify for the *American* Olympic team.

Some of the other runners were jogging back and forth along the straightaway, trying to get warm. Tesfay had never understood running as a way to get ready to run some more. He was always ready to run, could wake up in the middle of the night to find Robel was in trouble somewhere and run halfway around the Beltway to get him. At times like that, he would ignore his mother's disapproving looks, the questions about whether it was worth it that even Aunt Sophia began to ask after a while. Tesfay never questioned it when Robel needed help. Robel felt that for Habesha people, "family" was the end of an argument.

He had asked his mother once why, if Aunt Sophia was family and so well off, they had not moved in with her at once, or been rescued from the famine earlier by her money. His mother told him that Tesfay's father had wanted it that way. As a comrade of the struggle, he could not allow his family to escape the fate others were facing because they were fortunate enough to have a wealthy relative. He wanted them to fight to live, and through fighting to learn to love what they were fighting for.

The signal came for the runners to approach the starting line. Tesfay felt no nerves at all. To win or lose was in God's hands, just as to live or die was in God's hands. To be rich or poor. To choose a violin and become an Olympic hopeful, or to choose dirty blues and end up dead. All God, God, God. He had heard it so many times it didn't matter if he believed it in his mind. His body believed it.

The gun sounded and Tesfay shot out ahead. He could always tell within twenty strides what kind of a day he would have. Today was a good day, and he wanted to bury the field early, to leave them wondering for so long when he would drop off that eventually the question would slip from their minds, and they would view the race as a race for second.

As he rounded the first turn, he felt a familiar thrum vibrate through him. Someone in the Habesha crowd had brought a *kebero* and was beating it to spur Tesfay on. It was the wrong tempo for him, though. It was impossible to match up with it, because its two beats landed too close together for him to land left-right in time to the two thumps. He tried to just land on the left foot on the first beat, but that was too slow. He tried to land once between the downbeat and once on it, but that was too fast. He tried to ignore the drum altogether, to recall Brahms or Stevie

Ray Vaughn or the silence of slow death, but the *kebero* oscillated though him, blocking other music from his mind. He could not keep his pace, and he slipped from first to second, then to third, then to somewhere in the middle of the pack where he did not know what place he was in.

For lap after lap, he struggled to find his own rhythm again and to break out of the pack. He hated being in the middle of a sea of legs, where one misstep could end in tangled limbs and twisted ankles. Twice, he tried to move to the outside for a push, but each time, the *kebero* would increase the volume, and he would lose his pace and fall back into the pack.

That goddamned drum, that cycle that never stopped, never changed. Birth to famine to death, leaving your children behind to grow to famine and death. Running in a circle, hoping to get somewhere, ending up where you came from. Ba-bump.

He got nowhere through the fourth kilometer, or the fifth, sixth or seventh. He had never liked trying to come from behind in a race. He was either a frontrunner from the gate or that was that. Why couldn't that drum stop? He tried to remember Robel's playing in the basement, when, without ever having had a lesson, he did his best to keep up with *Pride and Joy*. Tesfay had wrinkled his nose at the looseness of the piece, and asked why Robel didn't learn to play decent music.

"Man, don't you know that Ethiopia is the home of the best jazz music in the world?" Robel countered. "This stuff is your culture."

"That's blues, not jazz."

"Whatever. Same thing."

Whatever. Blues. Jazz. Kenya. Ethiopia. Eight kilometers. Two to go.

Some of the field had fallen off, and he was somewhere around sixth place, in a group with several others competing for the top three spots and a place on the Olympic team. First place was a Kenyan who went to Stanford. Tesfay knew him from nationals. Nobody was catching him.

Tesfay wished he could have grown up longer in the mountains of Tigray, so he could have built his lungs up in the altitude. He tried to recall those highlands. Right before they had left, running in the mountains was the furthest thing from his mind. He had been too tired from hunger to run. But earlier, he remembered—perhaps his earliest memory—running with Azeb and his father and mother. It seemed like the happiest game they were playing, something they were making up on the spot. Tesfay had to tag Azeb, who then had to tag their father, who then would tag their mother. Their father teased their mother as he chased her, flipping her *netsella* down over her eyes as he ran past her. The game went on and on for hours, and they wandered deep into the wild. It wasn't until they returned to the village that night that Tesfay realized they had actually been running from the Derg, who had come to look for TPLA soldiers. The game was meant to keep the children from being frightened. Tesfay wondered what it would look like if he went back now, where the TPLA—now the EPRDF and in charge of the country—was said to be building all over Tigray.

There were 500 meters to go when Tesfay heard the shrill, banshee-like ululation from the Habesha women. The drum increased its pace. Tesfay realized that this was the *d'rub*, the final part of the song. They were trying to send him down the homestretch with everything they had left. Without needing to think about it, Tesfay fell in step with the faster rhythm. First place was out of the question, but he only needed to finish third to qualify for the Olympics. He had never saved this much for the end of a race before.

He pushed harder. The trilling of the women's voices became louder. It was a funny custom, Tesfay had always thought. It sounded like ghosts coming from out of the grave, but it was meant as a welcome. Women generally made that noise when a loved one returned after a long time. Life is short, and we love you. We are glad you made it back. He careened around the turn toward the corner of the stands where his people were gathered. The flags bounced along with the white clothes, and the colors bled together into all the colors in the world.

He ran for Ethiopia. He ran for America. For Robel, for his father. For whatever. He ran for the finish, for home.

Savage, Maryland

Toby's Sunday school teachers had attempted to resolve the problem of the existence of evil in the world by teaching him that in the beginning, all things were good, and evil had no independent existence; it existed only as good perverted. As an adult, walking with Ted Norman along the Wincopin Park trail near his home in Savage, Maryland taught him to suspect exactly the opposite: maybe at the heart of all things was an essential brutality that would pulverize us all sooner or later, and all that called itself good existed only as a fleeting resistance movement in a desperate, losing struggle against the evil that was the bedrock of all that was. That was why he decided to spend retirement taking a long shower.

The park was a landscape that lured you in with its veneer of gentility. But the soil was thinner than skin above hard volcanic rock, rock that jutted up without warning into salients that sprained the ankles of joggers. Roots from trees exposed by erosion cut across trails and sent hikers hurtling. Trees could not even push their roots more than a few feet into the soil, because they met impenetrable gabbro just a few feet below. They were forced to spread their roots sideways, and in a hurricane, the biggest trees were the first to fall. If you slipped near the Little Patuxent River, slick boulders punched your bones.

The ruins half-hidden off the trails had once housed rock quarries that made the Baltimore Basilica, and Toby had once assumed the boulders in the river were granite. That was before Ted taught him about gabbro: a dark, iron and manganese-filled rock that formed at incredibly high temperatures when Savage was the middle of the Appalachians and the Appalachians were higher than the Himalayas. In some parts of the park, chunks of it had rusted to orange, but in the river itself, the water had polished the boulders to a dark blue. Ted had given a walking tour of the trails to a group of seniors once while Toby tagged along. One woman was mesmerized by the blue rocks, and could not stop talking about them. Ted posted a sign on the bulletin board at the head of the trail, inviting walkers to "visit the now famous Wincopin Blue Rocks," and hoped it would become a tourist draw. The only tourists in Savage, however, were those who went to the old mill across the river from the park, now converted into boutiques.

Just ten feet east of the entrance to the trail parking lot was the driveway to Toby's house. Howard County could boast that it had preserved an inordinate amount of land for parks, but Toby had pulled off an even greater preservation trick: he had maintained his home in the middle of these public wooded lands, a lone private residence guarded from the world on all four sides by a land gashed by quarries and grown over again with pokeweed, mile-a-minute, and stilt grass. His property was surrounded by royal polonia trees struggling to reach the top of the canopy while poison ivy snaked around them, looking for all the world like fingers trying to pull the trees back down. Folks used to accidentally drive the 450 feet down his driveway by mistake, then make an awkward seven-point turn to head back up and find the trail parking lot. Toby let the smart weed at the front of his driveway grow wild, put up a "private property" sign, and hadn't seen a strange car since he couldn't remember when. If the trucks bringing construction materials to his house for the last five years hadn't been from his own company, they might never have found the place.

This was the terrain where Toby plotted his escape from the coming Ragnarok by building a bath house. Ayala, his wife, said it was a terrible waste of their golden years. She said her friend Daphne could get them in at a nice Jewish retirement home in Fort Lauderdale to spend the winters. Ayala was Jewish, which was enough for them both to qualify. Plus, there were the kids to see in New York and Chicago, and their oldest, Hannah, who, thank God, just lived up in Ellicott City, and would be happy for her parents to spend as much time as they wanted with her two little girls.

But the bath house was more than an old-age eccentricity to Toby. If anything could soften the bones on God's knuckles that were the bedrock of the Earth, it was water. Ted had taught him that hundreds of years ago, primitive scientists had looked for the perfect solvent and found that nothing dissolves like water. Water and time. Now that retirement was nigh, he had time. He needed water.

Fortunately, he had the means to get it. His property ran

down to the Little Patuxent. Years of government contracts building one classified facility after another for the National Security Agency had left him well-off, and after 9/11 had made him what some people might call rich. He knew how to build what he needed. The hidden nature of his property, combined with the ability to use power machinery operated by people whose paychecks he signed, allowed him to get it built without questions.

The deliveries to the house began two years before he sold the company. First, there were solar panels, then massive bar screens. He bought things as they were available and cheap, so materials did not always arrive in the order they would be used. The storage garage and eventually the backyard were overrun with what Toby assured Ayala would one day become an anaerobic digester. Great, round, blue tanks he called clarifiers sat in the backyard his deck overlooked, grass sprouting out from underneath like pubic hair.

The pipe system that ran to the river was built in his yard, then triple insulated. It would not go in the ground. It had to be installed with speed, so that its presence would not be detected. A great earth-tone tarpaulin to camouflage the pipe was draped over it, and at the point where the pipe pumped water in from the river, he had seven mighty gabbro boulders piled around the intake to conceal it.

Hannah scolded him for destroying the environment. "Water is a precious resource, and the county already faces droughts every summer. We can't even water our lawn more than two days a month."

But the whole point of the bath house was that it was in perfect harmony with nature. Toby was not taking up arms with the rebellion; he only hoped to dissolve himself in the water until the warring sides took no notice of him. He believed his plan would actually improve water quality in the river. He had made half of the outbuildings at the water reclamation plant along the river. He knew the process better than anyone. The plant was a point of pride for county planners; it took the shit and filth of half the county and cleaned it up to potable standards. You could actually drink it, although the latest plan had been to sell the water to the National Security Agency to cool its massive computers in its state-of-the-art cyber facility.

Toby would recreate what the county did on a smaller scale in his backyard. He didn't need to be able to remove tons of organic material. He was just bringing the water up one hundred and fifty feet to his bath house, heating it, running it over himself and then treating it before sending it back into the river. He wasn't asking for the Earth to surrender one drop of blood for him. Everything he took he would give back, better than he found it. He only asked to stand in the flow as it made the trip. He would even try to heat the water with solar if he could. The propane tanks were only a backup.

Ayala blamed their silver anniversary trip to Japan for giving him the idea, but in fact it went back to when Toby was nine. That was when he'd learned, a little earlier than most boys, that turning a daily shower from a dreaded chore to a pleasure was as easy as just not fighting it. He folded his arms in front of him, letting the water pool in the bowl his lower limbs formed, then listened to the gush slap against the acrylic as he raised his elbows up to the let the water go free. He repeated this process thousands of times, and watched as each time he returned his arms to the folded position, a rivulet would form from his left collar bone to his chest. Every time, it would take a different course across his body.

Like most boys, the shower was the first place he had masturbated, and thus shared his most essential substance with the world. But he seldom repeated the act in the shower afterward. He had heard of people who said they did their best thinking in the shower, but he almost never used that space for thinking. The shower was the antithesis of thought, of struggle, of ambition. He would work for sixteen, eighteen hours a day if he needed to. Whatever it took so that Ayala could hold her head up at synagogue. So she could give to the special collections, so their children could have the right music at their bar mitzvahs. So she could explain why she had married him instead of a nice Jewish boy. But no matter how many hours he worked, he never cut a shower short.

He had to hide the true nature of his creation from Ted. Ted was not just an amateur naturalist and a professional geologist, he was the head of the Howard County Development Committee, and if he knew Toby was pulling water from the river, he'd have to tell the authorities, no matter how clean it came out at the other end. So Toby just told Ted that the water was from his own well. That would seem reasonable enough if Ted didn't know Toby was planning to be in the thing for sixteen hours a day.

Toby got nervous once when Ted was looking over the construction, and Ted decided to head down through the overgrown grass to where his property met the river. It was something Ted had done a hundred times before—spontaneous need to see some new aspect of nature struck him, and he just followed it. When Ted saw the seven boulders in the stream, het let out a whistle.

"That is some beautiful gabbro," he said. Toby assumed that Ted would soon launch into his explanation of how gabbro was made, that it was formed at near a thousand degrees, while the quartz that popped up in strange places was the product of the last gasp of a volcano, formed at much lower temperatures. Ted had a habit of forgetting what lessons he had already taught. But Ted quickly retreated from the river when he saw the triangular head of a copperhead snake only three feet away from him in the tall grass.

"Huh. Isn't that something? I could go ten years here and not see another one of those. And there it was, right by me. If it had been a snake, it would have bit me. You get it?"

Toby tried to get Ayala into the spirit of it by having her design the interior. She would have none of it. She said if he was intent on being Beckett's Murphy, then it was Celia's job to get him to go out in the world, not to sit in the rocking chair with him. Toby had no idea what she meant. He had hardly read a book by choice in his life. Even the Bible verses he'd memorized as a child he'd done by just listening to the smarter students until he had it down.

So he was on his own for décor. He hired a pair of artists from Howard Community College who'd answered his ad on

Craigslist to paint a mural on the tile walls. They took his general directions for a pastoral scene of sheep in a meadow and improved upon it, adding flowing rivers, waterfalls, and a shepherd guiding the sheep. The waterfalls were placed so that the twelve shower heads spaced equally around the circular walls seemed to be pouring forth from them. Toby paid the artists enough to cover college for a year.

He retired the day his bath house was fully ready. He could stand (or sit, in a moveable, reclining, waterproof chair) beneath any one of the twelve fountains, or he could flip a switch, stand in the middle, and have all twelve converge on him at once. Another switch allowed the water to flow directly up in geysers from the floor. He did not go to Florida in November, but he also did not, for the first time in recent memory, get a terrible cold when the weather changed. He believed that humidity was the key to his health, and swore he could cure cancer if only everyone had a bath house like his.

Thanksgiving came, and Ayala went to Chicago to see Ben and his new wife. Toby brought a cooler filled with water and oranges and spent 68 hours straight in the bath house. With each hour, he rotated to a new spout, stared at a new section of his mural. He began to feel that he was in that scene with its rolling meadow, leaning against a haystack instead of a recliner, and the music from the water was the sound of his pipe he played as the sheep grazed.

Ted had told him that the woods in Wincopin Park had once been a sheep farm. The evidence was a long rock wall built over a hundred years ago. In the nineteenth century in Maryland, agriculture was almost all sheep-based, Ted reasoned, and so the wall had probably been meant as a pen for them. "Someone went to a lot of work to build this fence," he had noted. The fence still stood at the top of the steepest hill in the park, but every year the side of the hill gave a few more inches back to the river valley. Whoever had lived there had probably been happy to sell their land when the quarry wanted to buy it. The entire hill was crumbling into the river.

At Hanukkah, Ayala went to New York. Rosanne, who looked so much like her mother they could have been two sides of the same bagel, was nearly done at the New School. Toby planned to join them in New York: skipping Hanukkah altogether was too unforgiveable for Ayala to write off as pardonable eccentricity. The week before leaving for New York, however, something began to bother him about the mural in his bath house.

Black mildew had begun to grow on part of the wall. Naturally, Toby had understood from the beginning that mildew would be an enemy of his project, and he was prepared with the best cleaner he knew of. But the spot refused to budge. Toby viewed it as an assault of the darkness on his sanctuary of enlightenment, and though the spot had no particular shape, he thought of it as a dark wolf there to take his sheep. He fought back. He brought in UV lighting and shined it on the walls. He gave up the pleasure of his shower and opened up the doors for an entire day to let it air out. He tried one cleaner after another, then one sponge after another. Eventually, he painted over it, obliterating a butterfly alighting on a lily of the valley from the mural. The spot returned the day before they were supposed to leave for New York.

Ayala did not come to get him as he scoured the shed, looking for his power sander. He would shave the wall down until he found a layer of it that behaved. He was vaguely aware by midday that she should have come to get him by then. By the time the sun went down earlier than any day of the year, he knew she had left without him. Not to worry. He had fixed the spot on the wall for good. He would drive up alone tomorrow and surprise them all. They would see he had not truly lost his mind, how buoyant his mood was. The darkness had struck back against him, and he had weathered its blow.

He decided to get a good night's sleep and start off early in the morning. Might as well enjoy the repaired atmosphere of the bath house and take his rest in there. He lay back in his recliner, the warm air wrapping him better than a jacket, better than a blanket, better than the womb.

He awoke sometime in the middle of the night to find that the water in the bath house was a foot deep around him. He wondered if the drain pipe had frozen, but, although it was cold, he didn't think it was cold enough to freeze the water in the insulated pipe. He sloshed his way to the changing room, found his clothes from the day before, and entered into the night. His skin retreated from the December air back toward his organs. He stumbled around the back yard, searching for the flood light switch. When he found it, he peered into one tank after another. He tore the lid off the third tank and immediately realized what was wrong. Obsessed with fixing the spot on the wall, he had forgotten to clear out the sand filter. There was a lot of sand in Little Patuxent water. It could overrun a filter and jam the pipes in a matter of days. The exit flow back to the river must be clogged.

He had a snake for large pipes that was long enough to do the job, and, if he could find his larger drill, he would be able to drive it through, but he needed to feed it into the pipe from the bottom end in the river. He checked his watch. It was 5:15. The sun wouldn't be up for two hours. He would have to clear the drain at the very earliest moment, so that no morning hikers saw him doing it. He went back inside the house, and it felt like a strange place to him. What had Ayala done with it in the last three months while he had been in the back yard? Pictures seemed to be missing from the walls, although he couldn't recall which, and there was a scent of flowers he didn't know. Ted knew flora and fauna to some extent, but not well enough to identify a flower from its smell.

He found his rubber boots in his closet. They were in the same place they'd been when he'd worked construction. So were his work clothes. He thought he'd put those in the attic when he sold the company. His heavy winter coat was there, too, and the gloves that flipped down to let his fingers work were in the pockets. He made coffee and ate a piece of toast.

As he ate in the kitchen he'd had redone for Ayala's fiftieth birthday, he saw appliances he did not remember ever using. There was furniture in the living room that looked new. Everywhere, the walls had pictures removed, he was sure of it. There were paintings of flowers and covered bridges in their places.

Only the large wedding photo of Toby and Ayala remained in the hall by the front door.

It seemed strange, this couple surrounded by hints of a Jewish wedding. She wasn't kosher—he was free to put the cheese anywhere in the fridge he wanted—but being Jewish was still important to her. She'd raised all three kids to learn Hebrew and took them all to Shabbat on Fridays. Now Ben and Hannah had also married non-Jews, and Rosanne seemed to be pretty serious with what he assumed was a gentile lesbian. Why him? What had Ayala seen in him that made him preferable to the many Jewish boys who had, no doubt, been interested in her?

Half an hour before the sun was really up, when at last he could wait no longer, Toby pulled his North Face beanie over his head and crushed the frost-crusted grass beneath his boots as he walked down to the river. He stepped in carefully, knowing how slick the rocks would be beneath the water, covered by slime and the rot of the late fall. He pushed his hand in between the seven boulders, looking for the pipe. Normally, he would have found it by the feel of its flow, but that was blocked now. He pulled up one pipe, but it sucked at his hand, telling him it was the intake. His fingers were losing function faster than he had imagined. He made one more plunge into the water and raked the bottom of the river bed until his hands felt—if it could be called feeling—the end of the pipe, colder than the water it was in.

He perched himself on top of the pile of seven boulders. He would need to get his best grip and stand up with all the force of his legs to get the pipe free enough to run the snake through it. He braced his feet hard against the unrelenting firmness of the gabbro. One, two, three he counted. As he began his lift, a shock of a crackling noise shot out from the bush five feet away from him at the river's edge. Surprised, Toby tried to jump back, but had already begun his upward lift, and he got caught between jumping and lifting. He flew up in the air, legs carrying forward, and came down full force with his spine on a knob of the top boulder. His limp body slumped into the river, face still up. He caught the fleeting image of a deer bounding up the hill toward the safety of the woods. His body felt horribly cold for just a moment, but he was unable to shiver, and the feeling passed.

Ted had told him once that mountain goats would have done well here, and farmers would have done better to raise them than sheep. But the deer didn't do badly, either. Hunters had to shoot them in droves every winter, or they multiplied so fast they ran out of food and died the hard way. Funny the deer was so close, Toby thought. If it had been a snake, it would have bitten me.

What Every Parent Should Know About Brain Injuries in High School Sports

Concussions occur when the brain moves quickly within the skull.

Diane wondered what would happen to Mr. Woolwine's brain if she brought her dented drink tray with the Great Lakes Brewing Company logo down with sudden, disruptive force on his head. Mr. Woolwine's head was covered with artificially thickened hair made black and glossy with drug store color and combed with drug store gel, gel that dried into a hard crust that reminded her of her son's football helmet. Diane wondered if he even had a brain to protect, and if so, if it had ever moved quickly. What was the difference between a blow to the noggin and the way twelve vodka and tonics made him drop his keys on the dirty, red-and-blue checkered floor with a tinkling sound like bells at vespers?

One thing was sure: if Mr. Woolwine either put his hand near the hem of her skirt or offered advice on what to do with her son again tonight, she was going to find out. Most of the time, she reminded him where his hands should be without using her own hands, like she had done with her second son, Craig, when he was four and still sucking his thumb. Mr. Woolwine was a good tipper, a regular, and the only person at the Frazier who was still interested in what was beneath her skirt. But the position of male perspective on how to raise her sons was a position she had offered to one man and one man only, and when that man had showed no interest in filling it, she had made an irrevocable decision to leave the post vacant indefinitely.

When the brain moves suddenly within the skull, it changes how the neurons communicate with one another.

The boys' father gave her a concussion when they met, though Miss Tremblay, the cheerleading squad adviser, called it "getting her bell rung" and Diane thought she had fallen in love. She had been in the middle of a call-and-answer routine to the student body. *We got spirt!* (What?) *We got spirit!* (What?) *We got what... what...what...what...what, what, what, what, what, what, what.* She must have been swiveling clockwise with her hands on her hips during the *whats*, because that's what the bit called for, but she couldn't remember it. She didn't remember the team's doctor checking her out or the crazy talk her friends later told her she had made about the cat they had dissected in biology. Amy McPherson, the head of the cheerleading squad, giggled that Diane had tried to warn them all that the cat was working for Saddam Hussein. All Diane could remember was lying face up on the pebbly track that circled the football field and Andre D'Angelo standing over her, his bushy eyebrows and facemask hiding his eyes looking down on her. He seemed a hundred feet tall, a visored knight come to rescue her, although that made no sense because he had been the one to smash into her. But love insisted he was a knight. He spoke to her, but his voice sounded childish, his teeth unable to meet each other because of the mouth guard jammed between them.

"Wo. You all right? Really plowed into you there, didn't I?" He had accidentally bowled her over when he ran out of bounds after a play.

For a week, she was kept from doing any school work, although she still went to class, the puffy ball of chestnut hair pulled to the top of her forehead like the dot of a question mark as she floated airily from study hall to geometry. Words did not reach her, although from time to time it seemed that she herself was the subject being discussed. She wondered whether "ass over teakettle" meant something like "head over heels," and whether she was supposed to be thinking about such things. She passed Andre in the hall twice one day, three times the next, then seemingly he was omnipresent. He had so much hair everywhere: arms, head, eyebrows, sticking out his t-shirt top, even his face. She didn't know any other boys in high school who really looked like they had to shave. Around his neck, which reminded Diane of her Welsh Pony's, he wore a gold rope chain. Diane felt blood pound against her eyeballs when she saw it glitter in the hallway lights. It was love—she finally knew what it felt like to be in love. She felt sorry for everyone who still didn't know. Friday, she wore his jersey and she was cleared to cheer again.

You do not have to be hit directly on the head to get a concussion.

The Frazier, or "the Fraij" as most of its patrons called it, was often mistaken by those in the northwest section of Canton, Ohio for a garage: a flat, drab, one story beige brick building with a barely discernible hand-written sign. If asked to explain the name, most locals—who had never set foot in it— assumed that it was owned by a man named Frazier. For a whole decade after Diane started working there, curious visitors from Jackson Township and North Canton on their way to the Pro Football Hall of Fame would peek in, wondering if it was named for the TV character Frasier Crane from *Cheers* and *Frasier*. They were disappointed when they saw the raw, unpainted steel beams that broke up the symmetry of three rows of six tables and realized the bar looked nothing like the one run by Mayday Malone. Before they left, though, they always ordered a drink or two to be polite, and left Diane some of the best tips she ever got.

The bar was actually named for Smokin' Joe Frazier, whose picture was framed next to where two seams of paneling warped apart from each other. Frazier beat Muhammad Ali once and lost to him twice, the last loss coming in the "Thrilla in Manilla." The ref stopped that fight that Frazier refused to quit even when both his eyes swelled shut. Ali won, but he said the fight was "the closest thing to dying that I know of." After Ali retired, he shook like his own bobblehead doll, a victim of pugilistic brain syndrome from the many men he had beaten and the few who had beaten him. Tom Degenhardt named the bar for Smokin' Joe, because he hated Ali for being uppity, and said Frazier was the right kind of nigger.

Diane needed every tip she ever earned. She waited almost

until the end of high school to get pregnant. When she told Andre she was keeping the baby, she had meant for it to be her opening offer, but Andre did not counter. "Whatever you think is best," he told her, "it's your body." She struggled for a while to go to Stark Community College and worked at a video store while Andre managed to get hired on at Timken Steel. At night, Andre Jr. would stir in the crib in the corner of the bedroom Andre Sr. had grown up in, beneath Andre's poster of Barry Sanders.

"Could you get him, babe? I'm exhausted."

"Can't you do it, Di? You're a lot better at it than I am."

When Craig showed up two years later, she stopped going to class. Andre Sr.'s mother would not watch two children through both work and school. Diane asked Andre Sr. if he thought he might get promoted at Timken soon so they could move out.

"I don't know," he told her, and stuffed a finger of dip into his cheek, while Chris Berman's red face explained why the Chiefs would beat the Bengals. Diane picked up his spit bottle and threw it at him, but it missed and hit the wall, sending a spray of brown spit water fanning down the orange paint Andre Sr.'s mother had applied herself. The next day, the streaks of filth had randomly dried in the pattern of a large prairie animal, and Andre Jr. wanted to know where the cow on the wall had come from. Andre Sr. left for the Army two weeks later, before Diane used her last check from Blockbuster to buy a can of paint to hide the cow. He was punctual about sending child support checks of $328 on the first of every month.

It isn't uncommon for a player to hide a head injury, because the athlete wants to keep playing.

The Fraij and Diane both had weathered in fifteen years together. She could not understand why Tom wouldn't replace the paneling, or why he insisted that all waitresses wear skirts when she was past the age when a skirt helped her win tips.

"Honey, the girls who look good in them skirts ain't gonna work here. They're gonna work down at the Sports Page or Hooters, or they're gonna find a man in one of those bars and stop having to work. You just gotta make do with what you got," he told her when she brought it up. He had a dark toupee that he knew was terrible, and he tried not to move his head much when he talked to avoid drawing attention to it.

As the Fraij and her thighs fell victim to entropy, the collective wisdom of how a mother should view her son's relationship to football evolved. When Andre Jr. had first come to her in fourth grade, a permission slip held without folds or wrinkles in his hand, asking for forty dollars, she waited until the weekend, when the rates were low, to call Andre Senior. He was married again, and his new wife answered. Her voice seemed unnaturally calm, and she politely put Andre on the phone. When Diane explained that their son wanted to play football, and asked what he thought, he said that if Diane thought the boy was ready, then it was fine with him. He'd send the forty dollars.

The regulars at the Fraij and Andre's mother, whom Diane still needed for late night shift babysitting, had endorsed the idea enthusiastically.

"Aw, hell, he's a boy. He needs to play football," Tom said.

"It'll take the wild out of him. He'll leave it all out on the field," said Mr. O'Connell, a fireplace salesman who frequented the Fraij in those days between his first and second wives.

"Just the thing for a boy without a father around," said Andre Sr.'s mother.

"And you should sign up that other one you've got first chance you get," everybody added.

Andre Jr.'s first team was coached by Tom's son, Don Degenhardt. Tom was so proud of his son's team, he said he'd take care of Andre Jr.'s registration fee, and she could keep Andre Senior's forty dollars to use for cleats.

Don coached in Canton, not North Canton where Diane lived for the schools. Tom approved. "If he plays in North Canton, all he'll ever play against is white kids. He needs to know how fast those black kids can be from the start or when he gets to high school he'll never be able to catch 'em."

Andre Jr., it turned out, was as fast as anyone. But Don said what was really surprising were his hands. Andre Jr. could catch anything, even the wobbly "dead duck" passes thrown by ten-year-olds.

"Never seen anything like it in a kid his age," Don said. "Softest hands I've even seen."

It gave his team an advantage, since most teams at that level could only run the ball, never pass. Diane watched him from her fold-out chair on Saturday mornings, Craig sitting Indian-style in the grass next to her with his Pokémon toys spread out in front of him. She marveled when a pass would go up from a quarterback so small she could not see him behind the line of scrimmage, and the ball would tumble in a high, undisciplined arc until Andre Jr. controlled it at the bottom end, ripping it away from defenders and into his hands. She wondered where he had learned to do this.

"Craig, did you see? Your brother just scored a touchdown."

Craig made fizzing noises, spraying a little spit as he made a soundtrack to go with his story. Craig narrated the Pokémon battle as he directed it.

"Craig, don't you like football?"

Craig looked up, suddenly realizing that something outside his game was present. "Sure I do, mom." He continued on, chattering about fire types and hit points.

Concussions are hard to diagnose, because there isn't a specific test that can tell if you have one.

Diane's first sense of how good he was came in the fourth game of Andre Jr.'s junior year, when Hoover—named for the vacuum cleaners once made in North Canton, not for the president—played Glen Oak. He had just caught his sixth touchdown pass of the season from Jason Grovnar, and the band had not yet finished playing "Across the Field" when a whisper came to Diane from one of the fathers. *Someone is here from Akron to see Andre Junior. A scout.*

Diane pondered what this meant, her lips pursed tightly and still warm from her hot chocolate. Out of habit, she turned her head from the covered reserved seats that the parents sat in to the student section off to the left, scanning for Craig. It was harder than usual to pick him out in the crowd as tonight was a rivalry game, and the stands were fuller than usual. But she eventually saw him, pinned to the metal fencing on the far side of the bleachers, talking to his only friend, Scott Windham. They were both red-faced from laughing about something. Neither one showed any sign that they knew Andre Jr. had just scored. Diane turned to the father who had the news.

"Is Akron any good?"

After the game, Diane watched for Andre Jr. outside the locker room, while she took her turn manning the Viking Boosters' food station from which the players were fed after home games. She was handing out a foil-wrapped hamburger and could feel it was still warm through her thin latex gloves when she saw Andre Jr. emerge from the locker room in the middle of two of his friends. He looked up, but not at her. She followed his eyes to a tall, thin girl with protruding bones beneath her eyes. She was wearing number 93, Andre Jr.'s number, and the year Diane had graduated from Hoover. The girl smiled when Andre Jr. looked at her, a deep smile that covered the bony cheeks with flesh. Andre Jr. spoke a few quiet words to her, and she was gone. They didn't kiss, but she placed both her hands in his and they squeezed tight together.

"Who's your friend over there?" Diane asked Andre Jr. as he took his burger from her. His giant, loping form towered over her, and he smiled and quickly took a second. She found it hard to believe that all anyone could talk about when speaking of this huge child, with his stringy, blond hair combed in no way in particular, was how fast he was, how deft and soft his hands were.

"It's just Annie," he said, opening his first burger and cramming half into his mouth at once. He had only half swallowed when he added, "We're going to go see 'X Men' tonight. She's got a car."

Diane was going to ask at the Fraij on Saturday after the game whether Akron was a good team, and what it meant if someone from there was scouting her son. But it was not a good night for getting information out of Tom. As soon as Diane arrived for her shift and hung her Hoover jacket on a wire hanger in a corner, she knew he was drunk. He and Mr. Woolwine were arguing about something while a college football game played on the bar's only monitor. Diane hated when the college games were on. Although customers drank more during college games than pro, because the games were on Saturday and nobody had to work the next day, she hated hearing customers arguing over teams from colleges they had never gone to. Or worse, colleges they had gone to but she hadn't.

Tom, who was always a little brownish-red, such that Diane believed him when he said he had Indian blood in him, was now flushing crimson. He was leaning in toward Mr. Woolwine, and bright blood pulsed into his face with every word. He pointed and jabbed at the screen with all four fingers extended to emphasize each word.

"Pussies! Goddamned pussies! They're supposed to be god-damned football players, not ballerinas."

Mr. Woolwine retreated, leaning back in his seat. He put one hand in his gel-encrusted hair and ran it back. It wore the gel out in spots, and a racing strip of hair did not stay down.

"I'm not saying I like the rules," he started, evidently backing off of something he might have said earlier. "But these kids today, they start lifting weights when they're five. They take steroids and hormones and drink goat's piss and God knows what else. They can bench press a thousand pounds and still run a 4.4 forty. You can't let them run into a receiver when he's laid out to catch a pass and can't defend himself. They'll kill him. Just kill him."

Good. He was articulate. He must have just started drinking, meaning he still had a whole afternoon and evening of drinks ahead of him, with a dollar for Diane each time he ordered a new one. But his attempt to meet Tom halfway only seemed to have riled Tom up even more.

"Pussies! Bunch of goddamned moms trying to put their noses in football. You can bet that the Chinese don't have a bunch of moms making their kids wear tampons to play what-ever goddamned sports they play. No. They're raising them there to be men, which is why your kids will be speaking Chinese one day."

He noticed Diane for the first time, and jabbed his knife hand in her direction.

"Hey Di! Lift up your skirt and show him your pussy, so he

can see what every boy in America will become thanks to moms like you trying to make football safe."

There were only two other people in the bar, a younger couple. Maybe one of those lost Jackson Township couples. The man pushed himself half out of his chair, questioning Diane with his eyes whether he should do something. Diane saw at least a dozen bottles of Guinness clumped together on the bar, some with their labels picked at around the edges. Tom was really three sheets, going on three and a half.

"He's just like this sometimes," she said aloud, trying to calm the couple back into their seats. "It's part of the ambience of this place."

Tom launched himself toward Diane, staggered, caught himself on the back of a chair, and strode toward her again. "Don't disrespect me in my own goddamned bar!"

Diane's eyes watered from the alcohol fumes coming from his mouth. She felt a small bubble of his spit on her forehead.

"You women. You fucking women," he started again. "You've got no idea how to raise a man. You've got no toughness in you. Lucky my son got a chance with your oldest one, or he'd be a little doll-playing faggot just like that second one of yours, too stupid and scared to say a word to anyone."

She still had her purse in her right hand, because she needed to lock it up in the store room, so she swung with her left. She left her hand open, like she had with Andre Jr. when spanking him for stealing candy bars from the pantry. It was a wild, roundhouse swing, and the fatty heel of her hand landed on his ear. She could almost hear the ringing inside her own head. She stood with her left arm still extended to the right side of her body, where the follow through had taken it, and braced herself to be hit in return or fired. But Tom just laughed.

"Well, you've got some toughness in you. Guess that's why Junior's scored so many touchdowns." He patted her on the shoulder and walked behind the bar, past the calendar with the twins in bikinis on top of a Camaro.

If Diane hadn't believed in fighting fair, she'd have had better ammo than slapping Tom. He had another child besides Don, a step-son. After Tom had split with Don's mother, he'd taken in a white woman who'd had a son by a black man. She just needed a man with means to take care of her, and Tom knew it, but he loved that boy. Tom tried to raise him to be a football star, to do well in school so he could go to any college, but the boy had fallen into drugs and gangs and ended up dead at seventeen. "The black side got the best of him" was how Tom put it.

But Diane did believe in playing by the rules, so she never brought it up. On the way to the store room, she realized she hadn't seen Craig since breakfast.

To protect student-athletes, the rules now require erring on the side of caution, and any player who exhibits any of the signs of concussion shall be held out of competition until observed by a doctor.

Diane's mom and dad hadn't abandoned her when she'd gotten pregnant, but they hadn't been supportive, either. She assumed that they were still waiting for the elders at Faith Bible

Church to decide what the right thing for one of their members to do in such a circumstance was, and since decisions of the elders had to be unanimous, it was just taking some time to come to a final conclusion. Her parents came with her to the big McKinley game the week after the scout came to see Andre. Hoover almost never beat Canton McKinley, the school that fed Ohio State with running backs and safeties every year. But this year, the Grovnar-D'Angelo connection gave Hoover a chance. Even the elders couldn't deny football history.

When Andre Jr. hurt his knee in the McKinley game, she knew right away something was wrong. The game stopped. Players went to both sidelines and took a knee out of respect. Half a dozen overweight men circled around him as he lay on the ground. Mothers shouted for a pass interference call that hadn't come. Some turned around and looked sympathetically at her, shaking their hands together to indicate they were praying. Her own parents put their arms around her.

The Superintendent of Schools sent someone to take her to the ambulance. A cart took her son off the field, where he was then gingerly lifted onto a stretcher and loaded into the ambulance. Annie was next to the ambulance, her giant button with Andre Jr.'s football photo on it above her right breast. She asked if she could come along. Diane said that Annie should meet them at the hospital, because without her car, Annie would be stranded there. Annie yelled into the ambulance toward Andre Junior that she loved him, and Diane got in and the door closed as Annie looked in. Andre Junior said nothing, only closed his eyes and began to wait to hear the damage.

Rehab took a year. He went to special therapy for his knee while Craig started going to special therapy for a learning disorder. Andre Junior swore that he had regained all of his speed by the start of his senior season, but he hardly caught any passes. Jason Grovnar had graduated and the new quarterback, Deyvonne Reynolds, hardly threw the ball at all. When Deyvonne dropped back for a pass, he'd take a look, and more often than not he wouldn't like what he saw, so he'd just tuck the ball under his arm and run. Tom said all black quarterbacks were like that, which is why they never won Super Bowls and usually ended up going to jail for dogfighting. Akron didn't come to scout Andre Junior anymore. No schools did. The team lost three of its first four games.

When Andre Junior got his concussion, Diane did not know immediately that anything had happened. The only time she truly feared for her son on a football field was when he returned punts. On a regular offensive or defensive play, everyone was running all over the place, and nobody decided to hit anybody until the end. But on punts, all eleven players ran all the way down the field with one idea in mind—to smash into Andre Junior at full speed. The team needed him to field the punts, though, because of his soft, sure hands that never dropped the ball.

But the play when Andre's brain made a quick movement within his skull that interfered with its functioning wasn't a punt. He was barely in on the play at all. He came in at the last moment to help someone else make a tackle. Diane hadn't even seen anyone make contact with him. Another player had come sliding in and his knee accidentally knocked into Andre Junior's helmet.

Two plays later, Andre Junior was on the sideline, answering questions to a trainer who was putting his hands up to Andre Junior's eyes. Then Andre was back in. After one play, he came back out of the game, and somebody took his helmet from him.

An athlete can return to play once no signs of concussion have been evident for some time, although there is no exact time limit for how long one must be asymptomatic.

Give the state of Ohio credit, they were trying to make it safe for young boys to crack the skulls of other boys. It was now mandatory for anyone who had received a concussion to undergo neurological tests to monitor cognitive function before returning to play. Consequently, Andre Junior listened as a nurse read him the words *button, apple, wheel, frying pan,* and *paintbrush*, and he repeated four of the five words correctly. The problem with Ohio's test was that they had never measured Andre Junior's ability to remember five random words before his concussion. Was four out of five good for him? Nobody knew.

He had been injured in the eighth game of the year, just as the team was on a roll and hoping to pull a trip to the playoffs out of nowhere. But when Andrew Junior went down, they dropped games eight and nine, and were now 4-5 on the year. A losing record! Nobody could remember what that felt like. A bad year was to go 7-3 and just make the playoffs. A losing record did not happen.

The team didn't seem to really want him to play. They stood much to lose if Andre Junior were hurt again—possibly sanctions for putting a player in harm's way. They had nothing to gain. But Andre Junior insisted he was fine, and, other than forgetting "apple," showed no signs of lingering damage. So, the team deferred to Diane to make the decision. She made the mistake at the Fraij of asking Jack Geib, who had once been a paramedic, for his opinion. That led to Mr. Woolwine making his opinion known that if she were to let her son play after all that had happened to him and all that was wrong with Craig, she deserved to have her sons taken from her. This, in turn, led Diane to wonder if Mr. Woolwine's brain would joggle about its casing if she smashed a drink tray over his head. She took his ones without thanking him for each of the six beers she brought him that night.

As she took her jacket and slung her purse over it at the end of the night, Tom grabbed her by the elbow. She was afraid he had been drinking again. He held her around the elbow, and he seemed to be trying not to squeeze too hard but losing the battle to his own earnestness. He simply said, "Lee Woolwine's right. This game isn't worth it. Don't let him play."

Three days before the last game against Jackson, when Andre Junior was still saying he couldn't be part of the only senior class he knew of to have a losing record and when Diane still couldn't decide, Coach Spiegel suggested she talk to the school counselor.

Diane navigated through the school to his office during a break in classes when all the students were roaming the halls. It was her alma mater but it wasn't—Hoover had gotten a new building through a levy right after she'd graduated, and the new school was twice the size of the one she'd been to. She couldn't imagine Andre Senior in a place like this. Or herself, for that matter. It was entirely too big for them.

Mr. Coppolino, the school counselor, was clean-shaven, wore a sweater vest, and had a face that didn't wrinkle when he smiled. He asked Diane to explain her issue without further instructions. Diane guessed she should give the same pro-con list she had worked out in her head all week. On the one hand, it was Andre Junior's last game he'd ever play, he loved football, and he'd regret it forever if he didn't get one last chance to play. On the other hand, he stood a good chance of going to the Naval Academy next year. Annie had pushed him to study hard for his SATs and then to apply. She probably just wanted to get knocked up in more comfort than Diane had done at her age, but at least she had been good for something. Mr. Coppolino said "uh-huh" with a rising tone every time she paused.

"Well, that's a lot to think about, Mom," he said when she finished, laughing at himself for calling her that. "So, I guess you've got to ask yourself 'what are the risks and what are the rewards?'"

Diane squinted as though the sun had just peeked through the closed blinds. "I thought that was what I just did."

"Well, I can't make the decision for you. I'm here to help you to make the decision for yourself."

Diane did not understand. She repeated her pro/con list, and he still would not tell her what to do. He handed her a pamphlet on concussions in young athletes. It had a photograph of a teenage boy in a soccer uniform talking seriously with a man and a woman Diane assumed were his parents. She thanked him for his time and got up to leave. At the door, wondering how soon she would stop smelling his cologne after she left, she turned to him one last time.

"Would you let your child play?" she asked.

"Oh, no. My children don't play sports like football."

"And did you ever play football?"

"No. To be honest, I don't like it. I know that's not a very popular thing to say around this neck of the woods, so let's keep it our little secret."

Most people recover fully, although recovery make take longer the older the athlete is.

She hadn't been the best mom to Craig, she thought as she put her arm on the empty seat next to her that was never used at Viking Memorial Stadium. She loved him considerably, but definitely less than Andre Junior. Andre Junior's needs were easier to understand. After tonight's game, she would learn something about Pokémon, or about skating, or something else Craig was into. She would put more effort into working with his instructors to help him. It wasn't much to show for her as a mother, and it was late in coming, but it was something.

Andre Jr. would play his last game of football of his life. He had had a nice, but short, football career. Most kids never score a single touchdown in high school. Andre Junior had scored fourteen. Tonight, he would risk his body for his teammates whom he thought of as family but whom he would mostly never talk to again once he went to better places. His effort would be almost as selfless as it was stupid, and that was something. Probably good preparation for the Navy, anyhow.

Andre Senior did not come to the game. He had long promised that he would come to Andre Junior's last game. But as it got near, she felt that he was hoping Andre Junior would not be well in time for the game, and he'd be off the hook. In the end, he'd admitted that he didn't have either the vacation time or the money to come, and promised he'd make graduation in the spring.

Once, Diane had been run over by him and felt that she was in love. Once, she had sat with him and their sons on a couch in his mother's home and watched football on a Sunday and thrown a spongy Browns football to Andre Junior and played with Craig's baby feet. They had eaten barbequed chicken sandwiches. Diane had thought she was happy. And then she had worked like a dog for fifteen years to raise two sons, both of whom still had opportunities in front of them. It was more than something.

When Hoover stopped Jackson on their first drive, Jackson was forced to punt, and Andre Junior pedaled back to the thirty-yard line, awaiting the kick. Diane gripped the empty seat next to her. Goddamned punts. Only three things can happen on them, and two of them are bad. She gripped and pulled, wanting to tear off the arm and throw it onto the field to stop the game, until she felt a hand on hers.

"Is this seat taken?"

Tom was dressed in a pumpkin-colored turtle neck and dark

black slacks. He had tried to match the school's colors. Diane pulled him into the seat next to her by the arm.

"Hoover's got a chance to win this one," Tom said. "That quarterback of theirs has gotten better."

The Jackson punter booted the ball, and it tumbled end-over-end toward the sideline. Andre Junior raced to pick it off before it went out of bounds and snatched it just along the sideline. He scooted quickly up the field, picked up about ten yards, and ducked out of bounds when the Jackson cover unit closed in around him. The Vikings would take over with good field position.

She squeezed Tom's arm with both hands. He yelled for the offense to put some points on the board. Diane squeezed again, just glad to have someone there.

Mr. Sympathy

My father had what you might call acute sympathy pains, at least where Mom was concerned. When she was pregnant with me, she gained twenty pounds; he gained thirty. He shed the weight slowly, never really getting back into form until he topped her rotavirus with pneumonia that lasted two weeks. He claims he caught it from me, but my little pains and sicknesses never troubled him the way my mom's every ache or sniffle did. When it became clear that mom couldn't have more kids after me—her miracle child who came in her forty-second year—she suffered from temporary depression at the thought of never having another child to love, a depression she overcame with yoga and Prozac. Dad outdid her again by completely detaching from the one child he did have.

They'd been married all of two months before they realized I was coming along. Both had waited to build careers and check off their lists of places to go and accomplishments to accomplish before settling down, then met each other while celebrating their forty-first birthdays—only six days apart—on a Greek island tour. My father helped Mom back onto the boat when she came down with decompression sickness after a dive. He then got food poisoning that night at the hotel. Suddenly, they realized how perilously close they were to running out of time to start a family, and all the old items on their respective agendas were crossed off in favor of one, joint list. They were married in three months.

When I was born, fifteen months after they'd met at the Apollo Diving Center, they named me Corfu. When your first name is the name of a Greek island, and your parents aren't Greek, and you're not Greek, and nobody you know is Greek, and you live in Hartford, Connecticut, here are some of the names you might be called while growing up: Corfuck, Corfucker, Cockfu, Corkscrew, Bufu, and Tofu.

It isn't that my father had no love to give me. His love merely stayed balled up as potential energy, always waiting to be unleashed like a wound spring if I ever managed to be good at the thing he wanted me to be good at, to appreciate the book he wanted me to appreciate or excel at the sport he claimed he'd once excelled at. But I liked video games and needed three tries to figure out every math problem he ever explained to me at the dinner table. So the spring of his affection stayed locked in the loaded position until, I presume, it at last wore out.

We called the room where I did my homework the dining room, but we never did anything in it but my homework, which was always a group project. Meals we ate wherever the mood suited us. We left plates and silverware everywhere, and we'd round them up once a week in what amounted to a scavenger hunt.

This process where every feeling my mother ever had would

crash into my father and undo him through his own emotional incontinence played out over and over again. When Mom slipped on the ice and sprained her ankle, I saw dad limping around the house as he overturned the contents of the kitchen drawers, trying to make coffee for her while she propped her leg up and typed e-mails to donors to the non-profit she worked for. When I asked why he was favoring one leg over the other, he paused for a moment to look up from ransacking a colony of wooden spoons and said, "Was I?" When Mom worried about safety in our home, he installed security cameras in four locations. When she worried about mold, he bought a dehumidifier for every room. When that made her worry the house was too dry for her sinuses, my father had an automatic humidifying system installed in the duct work.

Even his essential political conservatism showed the gravitational effects of Mom's emotional life. He worked for an insurance company as a kind of actuary on steroids. He didn't just apply the formulas; he wrote the programs that uncovered the formulas in the first place. Insurance companies got rich off his skilled applications of probabilities and data mining. This didn't sit well with Mom, though, who believed these companies did so only at the expense of the vast majority of humanity who had no choice but to play a game by the house's rules. So my father would come home from a job where he'd rigged the game and write a blog where he revealed all the ways consumers could try to fight back against the house's tactics. He wrote about how to use zip code data in one's favor, how long exactly one could switch from cigarettes to chewing tobacco and be considered a "non-smoker" for a policy, how to stop lifting weights prior to a doctor's visit in order to drop BMI. In this manner, he undid each night the work he so painstakingly wrought each day, like those Tibetan monks who spend months building a Mandala one grain of sand at a time only to destroy it in the end.

My father was unwaveringly rigid, though, when it came to evidence and logic. Most of the disagreements I witnessed between them—which, I will admit, were far fewer than what my friends seem to have seen from their parents—had to do with the two American wars that lasted from my tweens to the end of my teens. Although my father was willing to admit that building democracy was either a smokescreen or a hopelessly quixotic *casus belli* for what was going on in Afghanistan and Iraq, he wouldn't join my mother in her knee-jerk assessments that the real reasons for the wars had everything to do with oil and enriching Halliburton. He would just say that the neo-conservatives had a flawed policy, but he could understand why they felt compelled to try to carry it out.

This kind of middle-of-the-road analysis never sat well with my mother, who enjoyed nothing so much as the deliciousness of being able to tag policies with the adverb "absolutely." "It is *absolutely* all about oil," or "Bush's foreign policy is *absolutely* racist," or "We *absolutely* are causing earthquakes to increase by dropping bombs on the Middle East." Her mind contained drawers of ideas where everything inside was well-ordered enough to find at a glance. She was either hot or cold. Either it was too dry in the house or too humid. When they reached impasses over these arguments, neither would budge for days. It would take some misfortune befalling my mom unrelated to the political disagreement for my father's instinctive sympathy to kick in and move him back in her direction.

My father's intolerance for shoddy thinking, coupled with his inherent sympathy for Mom, were what did him in, as much as the doctors will say it was esophageal cancer. Mom was suffering from a bout of laryngitis brought on by a change in the weather one fall. For the sake of peace in the house, she had taken over duties as my main homework tutor when I was in sixth grade, even in math, at which she was almost as bad as I was. I was so hopelessly behind that the remedial math classes I took were still easy enough for Mom to keep up. Bringing dad in was overkill, and he didn't have the patience to watch me struggle, anyway. He'd sigh every time I flipped the pencil from graphite to eraser in my hand.

The day my father filled in for Mom on account of her illness, he hung in there with me for a while, even though he was beside himself that I was still doing the same basic computations of fractions he'd been doing with me five years earlier. Several times, I heard him forcibly control his voice as he reminded me how to go about the four operations.

"Three rules, son. There are only three rules. Addition and subtraction are the same rule: find the LCD, add or subtract across the top, keep the bottom. Multiplication is the easiest. Just multiply across the top and bottom. Division is almost as simple but with one extra step. Invert first, then multiply across. Nothing could be easier."

But I had an unconscious tendency to change math problems

from the problem in front of me to the problem I wanted it to be. If, for example, I had an addition problem to solve with an eight in the denominator, my mind immediately multiplied it—I find multiples of eight aesthetically satisfying, for some reason. So I would multiply across, simplify, and get the wrong answer. My father endured this for as long as he could, but eventually, I had profaned so monstrously his sense of the world, his belief that any rational person with patience and commitment could master mathematics, that he screamed at me longer than I thought I person could scream without running out of breath.

When he was done, his words continued to bounce off the walls, their intensity dying according to a logarithmic function with each pass. My ears readjusted to the silence. One wall of the dining room where we did homework was covered by small, ornamental mirrors. I wondered if sound reflected off mirrors the way light did. Would the echoes come back inverted, my father praising me for my persistence with something I found difficult?

Later, after he calmed down, he apologized for his outburst. His voice was ragged and had lost range at the high and low ends. He'd shouted himself hoarse. His voice stayed in that croaking state for days, weeks, long after Mom had recovered from whatever minor ailment had been troubling her. Mom and I both believed his lack of voice was related to feeling bad about how he'd berated me: *Why can't you get this? What's wrong with you? There are four-year-olds who get this! I don't want to hear that you're 'just not good at math.' What if someone said 'I just can't get reading and writing?' You'd call that person illiterate, and you'd be right! That's what you are, son, illiterate. You're illiterate with numbers. If you felt the shame at this you ought to feel, you'd have figured this out by now.*

We were so convinced his lingering throat-clearing and forced syllables were symptoms of an emotional malady that by the time we finally forced him to go to the doctor, his cancer was already too advanced to halt. Not that the doctors didn't try; they used their weapons of mass destruction, both chemical and nuclear, but the war effort became a slog that killed a lot more of the ordinary citizens of my father's body it was meant to protect than it killed the terrorist cells inside of him. The only noticeable difference their strategy wrought was to ensure my father spent the last few months of his life unable to speak.

During those months, Mom had what you might call a reverse sympathetic reaction to dad's condition: the more his heavy muteness filled the house, the more compelled she felt to talk ceaselessly. She'd chirp about Lesbos, then flit to another branch and ask whether he thought he'd be able to go back to Greece for one last trip. Before he could sign his way through an answer, off she flew again and alighted on the twig of possible alternative treatments. He'd probably gotten his cancer from the scalding coffee he'd poured down his throat for years—turns out hot water is kind of a carcinogen when running down a human's pipes. But Mom was convinced he'd somehow heal himself by switching to herbal tea.

I know it must have hurt my father to bear that kind of talk in silence. He couldn't tolerate pseudo-science. But after he'd tried for a few days to sign or write or text his responses to everything, he seemed to lose the will to keep trying. He simply bore most of what Mom said to him in silence, giving her only an occasional nod.

Knowing time was limited, I determined I would accomplish one thing to make him proud of me before he died. If I had surveyed my limited pool of talents, looking for the skill I possessed in sufficient quantity to put me within striking distance of a distinguished accomplishment, I might have aimed at volunteering for a social cause. I was surprisingly adept at Spanish, supplementing what I'd learned at school with a regular dose of telenovelas on Univision. I might have tried to help recently arrived residents of Hartford with tax returns or voter registrations or job applications or any of the many things they no doubt could have used help with. My father would have liked that. He believed in giving others a hand up.

Instead, I chose math. I was a junior in high school then, and about to take my SATs. I decided I would ace the math section. If I'd been better at math when I made that decision, I would have immediately rejected this idea based on its imposing improbability on multiple fronts. Not only was I still playing around with dummy math, not yet having really even tackled algebra, but the timing was all wrong. On the one hand, I had only a little less than three months to learn years of SAT-level math I'd failed to tackle with all the years I'd had so far. On the other hand, it would be weeks after the test before I had my scores. I didn't know if he had that long.

Not knowing the odds, though, I swung for the fences and decided to try to master math. My first day was the worst. Starting with where I was in the textbook from my dummy math class,

I decided to do every odd-numbered problem in the book, checking with the answer in the back. If I didn't get it right, I'd go back and keep re-working the problem until I did. But I missed so many problems with the first assignment, it took me until well into the evening to finish. I'd gotten no further than one night's homework. I hated exponents. What did a negative exponent even mean? I still couldn't get three of the questions right by the time I gave up and went to bed.

In the morning, I went to gather my crumpled sheet of problems to put in my bag, when I saw little red marks on it. They were meant to be circles, but each near-circle began at six o'clock, spun too quickly around counter-clockwise, and ended up above where it had originally begun, forming something between a lower-case "e" and a tadpole. Each tadpole encased the step in my work where I had begun to go wrong. In my car in the parking lot in the fifteen minutes before school, I corrected my mistakes. In third period, I handed in a nearly perfect, if very smeared, assignment.

That night, when I struggled again with my homework, I found my father sitting up on the couch, watching the Mets squandering a giant lead in the playoff race and all the millions of dollars they'd spent to build that lead. Baseball was one of the few things that got him vertical by fall of 2007. He'd played at Georgia Tech and had later been deeply disappointed in me when I failed to play past nine years old.

I handed him my math problems with neat little stars consisting of five triangles around a hexagon by each of the ones I hadn't been able to figure out. I placed a large coffee table book underneath my work to steady his writing and handed him a red pen. His right arm he had once pitched with shook beneath the weight of the book. Barely taking his eyes off Billy Wagner, he effortlessly dashed off his tadpoles in the places my calculations had started to go off-track and handed the paper back to me.

I took the work back to the dining room table, redid the six problems, corrected four of them, then brought him the two that still stumped me. By then, the Mets had blown another game, and he pointed the remote wildly all over the room before he could finally control his arm enough to turn television off. He slapped the couch seat next to him, his clammy hand sticking to the faux leather, and I thought he was having a seizure before I realized he was telling me to sit down.

I sat, careful not to sink too far into the cushion for fear of my weight sucking him in and toppling him over. He whipped the paper over onto the back and did each problem, slowly and from memory. He never once had to turn the paper over to check what the problem had been. He was remarkably still, numbers somehow orienting his addled nervous system enough to focus him in one place. He returned my work to me and went back to lying down and watching the ceiling. I turned the paper over and back twenty times or more, checking my process with his, finally finding the mistakes. Before bed, I managed to get through a second lesson in the book in the same manner. When I brought him my mistakes, he sat back up, scratched out his tadpoles, worked the problems on the back, and slumped back down when I was finished with him.

We continued like this for several nights, the Mets blowing

their lead, me pushing through as much math as I could manage. On the weekends, I did math from the time I woke up until I went to bed. One weekend, I discovered coffee and didn't go to bed at all. No matter how sick dad was, when I brought my math to him, he rose like Dracula from his coffin, left the blood-marks of his corrections on the page, worked through the ones that had stumped me on the back, and returned to his resting position as soon as I was satisfied. It didn't matter if he was sleeping. If I sat down next to his feet, however gently, he would rise and hold out his hand to take my work from me.

I finished my assigned math book for the class at school and ordered a real Algebra book from Amazon. When it came, I almost didn't get any math done that day, because I was stroking the glossy cover of the book, not believing I was really about to study something so exotic. It was like seeing the Eiffel Tower at an advanced age after having put off a dream vacation for decades. My father shocked me that night by shuffling into the dining room on his own and asking me with shrugged shoulders where my work for that evening was. I opened the book and realized I already knew most of what was in the first chapter.

When the Mets finished one of the greatest September collapses in baseball history, I thought it would be the end of my father. He had to stay lying down while he fixed my work. His writing had become so shaky, I couldn't decipher it enough to know where I'd gone wrong. When I came home from school one day, there was a girl sitting at the homework table in the dining room. She was wearing a sweatshirt from my high school, but I didn't recognize her. I soon learned that this was because she was one of the smart girls who spent half her day being bused to the local community college, having already exhausted all the calculus courses the school had to offer. She had a rounded jaw and dark hair with bangs cut in a line as straight as a book end across her forehead, making her look like my grandma in old pictures from when she was young.

She told me she was my math tutor, that my parents had hired her that day at twice her normal rate, stating it was an emergency. My father was sleeping fitfully on the couch; Mom was nowhere in sight. I thought it was strange she hadn't been there to introduce me.

Emily took over for my father from that day forward. She was nearly as impatient as he was, drumming her fingers quickly on the table if I took too long to answer a question. Displaying even then my talent for recognizing hidden value that I now utilize as a junior portfolio analyst at Saxon Brothers, I saw the latent beauty beneath her bangs. I didn't want to disappoint her or for her to think I was stupid. With her, I felt something I had never felt, not on a baseball field or a classroom or anywhere. I was afraid to fail. If my mind began to drift off, fear pulled me back. It was like listening to an airline attendant give crash instructions as the plane was going down rather than while taxiing on the runway.

What also helped keep me awake was the smell of Ben-Gay coming from my algebra book. Emily noticed it first, wrinkling her nose and dabbing at her eyes. I was used to the odor, as my father rubbed himself with liniments to cope with aches, but this odor was coming from right beneath me. I noticed that some of the pages in my book were wrinkled and flipped through. The back of the book had greasy, odorous fingerprint marks on several pages.

That first night, I continued to study long after Emily left. I wanted to work ahead so I knew the next day's lesson ahead of time. As I scratched away, wearing tiny grooves into the table below the paper as my Hot Pockets grew cold on their plate, Mom silently padded down the carpeted steps, came into the dining room, and laid her hand on my shoulder.

"How did you like Emily?" she asked.

"She's fine," I answered, feeling perturbed to be interrupted even for a second. "Why didn't you tell me you were getting a tutor?"

She picked up the plate of Hot Pockets. "Your father and I didn't agree at first. He sent me a text message that he can't keep tutoring you, so I said I would take over. He almost broke his own nose letting me know that I can't handle it anymore, that you're doing math I can't help you with. I started to disagree, but he somehow managed to get himself up off the couch, come out to the living room, grab your book, and shove it in my face repeatedly. I had to admit, when I looked at it, that I didn't even know what a quadratic equation is. So we got Emily."

That explained the Ben-Gay in my textbook. I tried to picture my father pushing the book at my mother. I remembered him pushing a bat into my hands over and over at the park one day when I kept trying to drop it, saying I didn't want to play anymore. "Quit at this, quit at everything," he'd said to me.

"You know, I hate to say it, but it's been kind of nice having

Dad not be able to talk," I said to Mom as she took my plate to the kitchen. "It's been maybe the best time we've ever had together."

She paused at the door, the plate held in one hand like the blind figure of justice holding her lamp. She'd had to be the buffer between my father and me so often, we'd kind of formed our own little club. Now, she was being forced to endure her son and husband—and now her son and a girl his own age—colluding in a language she did not understand.

"You know, when your father used to feed you as a baby, he was one of those people who would mimic eating in the air with his mouth while he was trying to get you to take the spoon," she said. "I used to tease him about it mercilessly, and he'd get so mad, but he couldn't help himself. There'd be you, carrots or squash or peas spilling down your chin while you tried to figure out how to gum down your food, and he'd be there in front of you, just biting down and chewing away on nothing."

She looked down at the remains of the microwave dinner I'd made.

"He can't help it," she said. "He sees the way people ought to do something, and he just wants to get in there and do it for them. I'll get you something better to eat. Sorry. I should have come down earlier."

My father held on as long as he could while Emily took over his duties. I was still able to make use of him as a sounding board. When I was trying to memorize formulas of geometric shapes, I'd pace back and forth in front of him as he lay on the couch, reciting one after another. If I got one wrong, he'd emit a phlegm-filled bellow. I'd check my flashcard and say it right. When I struggled with understanding what an imaginary number even meant, I'd talk it out with him. If I said something that didn't jibe with mathematical logic, his eyes would raise up at me while he lay on his side.

"No? Not right?" I'd ask him, and then I'd start over and try something else.

In the middle of the long Veteran's Day weekend, which I'd hoped to make use of to cram straight from quadratic functions into trigonometry, I had something of a breakdown on Saturday night. Suddenly, numbers made no sense to me. What did they even mean? Were they real? How could zero mean nothing and also still be a number? Every lesson I'd struggled through for two months suddenly came to me all at once, all vying for brain space at the same time. My father, who had fallen asleep as I paced the floor, woke at one point long enough to throw my math book at me. I went to sleep. When I woke up, all the questions had dissolved, and math made sense again.

I kept late nights. I slept in school sometimes; I was so far beyond what we were doing in there, it made little difference. If I started to drift off while Emily was talking, she'd rap her knuckles loudly on the table to make sure I was paying attention. Sometimes at night, I'd start to fall asleep until my head dropped into my textbook, and the burning vapor from Ben-Gay would startle me awake again.

On the day before the SAT, which was a week after Emily and I had split time at one another's houses on Thanksgiving, my dad was fading fast. Hospice was spending time at the house by then, and they were more concerned with keeping him from feeling pain than keeping him breathing. I leaned in close to tell him I was going to make him proud. The smell of adult diaper and bad breath nearly knocked me down, but I asked him to hold on a little bit longer.

"If you make it to Christmas, we should know my scores by then." He lay there, his mouth flaring open and shut, open and shut, like a fish, just taking in air.

He died while I was taking the test. He was never sentimental about things. He knew that if he held on long enough for me to just take the SAT, the result would be the same whether he was there to hear about it or not. My mom, whom I had hardly needed at all for the months of studying, suddenly became the most important person in the world to me, mostly because of how much I knew she needed me. I'd need her again in spring when Emily broke up with me right before prom. I'm not ashamed to admit there are times when a boy just needs his mom.

Mom got remarried in 2010 to a younger Yankees fan. He has three kids, some of whom are still little enough to need mothering. When she sneezes, he doesn't even say "gesundheit," but he does laugh a lot. All of his children love sports.

In college, I had a few girlfriends, none of whom were long understanding of dating a math major who was so serious all the time. Same thing with the girls I've dated since coming to Saxon Brothers. Sooner or later, I assume, I'll get to a level where I'll know I've done enough with my life to be ready to commit more to one of those relationships. When that happens, whoever I'm with at the time will pass from being a place holder to someone whose true value I recognize. When the time is right for something, it tends to all happen in a rush.

The Strongest I've Ever Been

Bill hoped the cloud from the spray deodorant he had borrowed off the shelf wouldn't show on the security cameras. He needed deodorant because he hadn't packed it in his gym bag, and after he'd finished working out with Tony that morning, he didn't feel like going home. So he picked an aerosol deodorant, figuring it wasn't that unsanitary to use and put back, and he chose a spot in the cosmetics department to put it on—right behind a cardboard cut-out display of three teenage girls of different races having a pillow fight. The cut-out was just the back of the display; in front were pink trays of mascara and eye liner. Bill hated the display, because it blocked half an aisle in the cosmetics department. Plus, the product was crap; three customers had already brought it back, one of whom continued to berate Bill's ability as a manager even though he had given her a full refund. Alisha, the head of cosmetics, had complained more than once about the display and everything that went with it.

Bill had showed up more than an hour before opening time to get a head start on the reconstruction of the seasonal display. He knew the district manager would have him rework it when he came in later. Phil always came in on Wednesdays, because that was his half-day, and Bill's store was the closest one to Phil's house. Phil's directives were erratic; he had no consistent aesthetic when it came to displaying merchandise. One Fourth of July, he'd put 36-can coolers next to ice packs based on common functionality, and the next he'd put insecticide next to lawn ornament American flags because he thought the colors went together. Bill more than half guessed that Phil just ordered endcaps changed because he had to fill the time and making changes made him seem necessary.

Every year, as he measured the height needed to fit pinwheels between shelves, Bill thought that he wouldn't be back next year, but this was his eighth summer with Drug Barn. Today, he was still full of endorphins after the gym, and he wanted to keep the momentum going, so he'd spent the morning making his best guesses about Phil's tastes, sliding stacked boxes of Epsom salt from one end of the first aisle to the other to make room for sparklers, jabbing random items onto peg displays and switching between seventeen- and nineteen-inch shelves. The sound of the grit on the floor as he scooted heavy cardboard over it irritated him. Why didn't Andy mop the floors before he ran the buffer over them? Now there was dirt blended into the wax, smearing the shine on the checkered tiles.

He tried to remember where he'd left his green canvas notebook so he could jot down a note to himself to talk to Andy. He also wanted to add a note about including side planks in his workout plan. He was so busy thinking about his workout, he almost ran into Alisha, who had come in silently.

She didn't usually arrive so early, because she had to take her son to daycare. If she was in early, that meant her boyfriend must have been out of work again and staying home with the kid. Bill knew more about Alisha than any other employee, both because they'd been together at Drug Barn so long and because her son happened to also be the son of Tony, his best friend and lifting partner. They weren't together—never had been, really—but Tony was involved as a dad.

She wasn't the kind of girl who looked too long in your face. Not that she was shy; she was like a poker player who didn't want to give away her tells. Bill had the impression she could read him in the second it took her to look him over, though. She had a thin layer of sweat on her forehead beneath the bangs she had swept sideways. Her hair had been every color Drug Barn stocked. Today it was one of those reds that she'd probably tell him was dirty blonde. You couldn't settle the debate by looking at the box, because hair colors didn't have names the way fingernail polishes did. They only had numbers.

As soon as her eyes darted away from his, they settled on his green notebook he had left sitting on top of a cutout of shaving cream. She reached for it with her thin left hand, two fingers kept slightly apart from the long habit of holding a cigarette. A silver chain flopped down from above the nobs of her wrist bone and came to rest on the light veins on the back of her hand. Bill felt a surge of horror as she started to open it. He wanted to rip it from her hands, but to act like it mattered would be to surrender power, and he resigned himself to playing out the inevitable scene to follow as coolly as he could manage.

She turned the canvas cover over. He'd just bought the notebook two days ago. Managers always carry little green canvas books with them to take notes, but Bill also kept his workout diary in there. There was only one entry in the book so far, and he knew she was reading it now.

July 2nd 2014

Squats

135 X 8

225 x 8

275 x 4

305 x 4

315 x 4

330 x 4

225 x max effort

135 x max effort

Romanian Dead lifts

70 x 10

80 x 10

90 x 10

Calf Raises

Four sets of 12—change foot position after each

Then, there was the note of encouragement. "Remember your goals!" Bill imagined this was behind the hint of a parabola from her mouth. Alisha had worked with Paige, an obese woman with a stomach condition that gave her gas, for four years, and never had Alisha uttered a word of mockery. But earnestness, Bill had learned, always earned her derision.

She crooked one eyebrow toward him up from the book, which she still held open, although by now she must have read all there was to read. Bill waited. There was only one thing she would say.

"So," she sang, putting the book down at last, but leaving it open on top of the shaving cream, "are you the *strongest* you've ever been?"

It was a joke that went back as long as they had both been working at Drug Barn. They had been brought on together in the same week during a hiring spree, after a group of other kids from their high school had been fired all at once for shoplifting. Bill got in by a good word from Tony, the only part-timer who hadn't been fired. Bill and Tony would interrupt blocking and facing the food aisles to pour over the latest *Muscle and Fitness* they had plucked from the magazine rack. They'd pick the best of Ronnie Coleman's workouts and plot together to add bent lateral raises to their routine to pack on mass to their lats.

One Thursday night, when all hands were required on deck to get twelve pallets from stock room to shelf in five hours, Bill and Tony were finishing up in the automotive aisle, and Bill leaned on the pallet jack with its tongues still wedged beneath the splintery wood. He stretched his calves and felt a satisfying burn.

"Man, today was squats, Tony."

"Hm." Tony ripped open a box of Turtle Wax with his white box cutter.

"It was awesome. I did 350 six times. I was the strongest I've ever been."

He heard a suppressed chortle behind him. Alisha had blue hair she kept short and swept to the side, like a boy. Tony, his box cutter sliding open in his fingers, looked up. Bill spun around, his hands still resting on the pallet jack handle.

"You say that every time," she said, her long face smiling.

"Say what?"

"That you were 'the strongest you've ever been.'"

Bill couldn't remember having ever said it before, but it sounded like something he would say. He took lifting seriously.

"Well, I was. I squatted three hundred and fifty pounds today. A lot of guys who weigh two hundred can't do that. I did it at one-fifty."

"But do you really need to say it? I mean, if you keep lifting weights, you're bound to get stronger, right? So wouldn't you be the strongest you've ever been, like, every time?"

"It doesn't work like that," Tony answered for them both. "There's plateaus. You can get stuck for a long time at the same weight. You can even go backwards. To keep getting stronger takes a lot of dedication."

"If you say so," she said, and disappeared in the direction of the pharmacy.

From then on, if she caught the two of them together anywhere near the magazines, she'd warble, "Were you the *strongest* you've *ever* been today?" Those were the days when Tony and Bill first started working out together, which lasted until Tony left for college. Without ever really meaning to, Bill became head of receiving, then manager trainee, then assistant manager, while

Alisha had stayed on to become head of cosmetics after she'd had Tony's baby. Bill kept lifting by himself with Tony gone, but was too embarrassed to buy his creatine and nitric oxide supplement at Drug Barn if she was in the store.

"I haven't been the strongest I've ever been in years, Alisha," Bill told her, snapping the green book shut on top of the shaving cream. "That's the whole reason I'm doing this. I need to get back there."

"Well, don't hurt yourself," she said, and turned toward cosmetics.

"Hey," Bill said, and then regretted saying it. He was never sure what he was feeling around Alisha. Was he about to ask her something now to keep her from going, or because he needed to as a manager? Or was it both? And why did it always seem that she knew better than him?

"Hey," he said again. "That display. Let me know if people keep bringing the makeup back. Phil's here today, and I can let him know."

"Okay," she said, and hiked her purse over her shoulder before turning again to go.

Phil was in a good mood. He suggested only light alterations to Bill's seasonal display. They walked the floor together, then surveyed the toilet paper and tissues that were overflowing in the stock room. By eleven, Phil looked like he was getting ready to leave. Maybe he had a golf game. Bill was dying to take a piss, but Phil never seemed to need to have physical needs, and Bill didn't want to ask to leave while Phil was giving instructions. The creatine and post-workout protein shake were really straining to get out.

"Oh, one more thing before I go," Phil said. Bill tried not to look at the tuft of hairs that sat in the middle of his otherwise bald crown. "There might be an opening soon at the New Philadelphia store. We're opening a new store in Carrolton, and we're moving Tracey from New Philly to be the manager there. You could have your own store. Not for sure yet, but something to think about. Anyhow, I've got fifteen minutes to make my tee time."

The next day, Bill was encouraged by the bench press numbers he was able to write down in his green book. He had gone to 275 with his heavy set, which was far off his mark of 340 from six years ago, but still better than he'd hoped, and better than anyone else in the gym could do. What Bill did not write down, because he was afraid it would be discovered by Alisha, were his feelings about what some guys at the gym had said afterwards.

Bill was used to the shift in volume at the gym when he went for his heavy set on bench. The clack of dumbbells being reset in the rack or partners encouraging one more rep out of their gym mates would simultaneously hush, as the entire free weight section fell into a spontaneously choreographed waiting. Only the far-off whir of the cardio machines could be heard, and the unspoken question on everyone's lips was *can this little guy really lift that much weight?* The first rep was always the scary one, when even Bill himself wasn't sure the bar would really go back up once it hit his chest. Once it did, though, he fell into the rhythm of

Tony's voice counting the reps from one to eight. He could sense the eyes on him from all around, feel as they went from disbelief to envy, all the time knowing that if Tony's voice said *six*, then the bar would go up one more time. Tony had that effect of making you believe you could do it. He called out the eighth and final rep as soon as Bill's elbows broke through the crux. The gym stirred back to life again. At the bench next to Bill and Tony, two men a foot taller than Bill shook their heads. Bill saw the gesture, and assumed it was respect until one wearing a black Under Armor shirt with matching shorts snorted at Bill.

"Must be nice to have such short arms. I could lift that much if I had arms like that."

Bill had heard this before, especially back in the days when he was competing. He had a response ready.

"You've got longer levers, but you've also got room all along those levers to build muscle. You can't use arm length as an excuse. Ryan Kennelly is six-two, and he benches over a thousand."

"Look, you little shit," the black shirt responded, much angrier than Bill expected, "it's fucking physics. Smaller lever means less effort to move the lever. Did you even go to college?"

Bill cocked one eyebrow. The man's tone was in that gray area between what gym rats considered joking around and a challenge. Bill had taken down bigger people as a wrestler. He considered taking a step toward the man, aggressively drawing an imaginary chart with an x and y axis on the man's chest and demonstrating the weakness of the short arms hypothesis using linear regression. Go to college. Anyone with a math book with the answers to the odds in the back could figure it out.

But Tony answered first. "Guys. He benched 275 eight times. He did that by training hard. Nobody needs to take shit away from him for doing that. You train as hard, you'll do the same thing." Tony was as tall as both of them, and wore his gray police department sweatshirt he'd had since the academy. He neither flinched nor took a step forward or back. The man in the black shirt put his hands up in front of himself and waved off what he had said.

"Hey, man. No offense," he said. "Just wish I could lift that much is all."

People always saw things Tony's way. He'd had a voice like a drill instructor's since he was fourteen, and he'd been persuading people with it since before he was even tall. In high school, it had been a blessing to be his friend, but also a curse. When Alisha had first started teasing Bill, he'd hoped her teasing was flirting, and that eventually the two of them would end up using the back corner of the stock room away from the cameras together. But it had been Tony who'd ended up there with Alisha. Tony had paid for it: he only went to college for two years before heading to the police academy. He sent their seven-year-old child support every month. But Bill still wished he had been able to visit the stock room with her.

It had been Tony's idea to revive their workouts. They'd met at a pool party at Tony's house on Memorial Day. He'd just bought a colonial in one of the new allotments north of Market Street. Bill hadn't seen Tony since Christmas, and it had been slow getting conversation going. His wife, Jaimie, hung at his side, wearing a yellow sundress draped over a bathing suit, which she managed to make look elegant. When Bill took off his top to jump in the pool, she'd embarrassed him by gasping "Oh, my God! Look at those muscles!"

Bill confessed he'd been slacking at the gym lately. It was starting to creep into the rest of his life, too. He wasn't as focused as he should be. So Tony suggested they get back to working out together. They would start on July 2nd, the middle day of the year, and call it a mid-year's resolution. It would be a little tricky to synch up, because Tony worked nights, while Bill rotated between days and nights at Drug Barn, but they could meet at 5:30, before the store opened and right after Tony got off shifts.

Bill stretched his left arm back over his head by putting his right hand on his left elbow and pulling. He felt a good tug. His muscles were already sore, and he hadn't even slept on his workout yet. It was 7:30 P.M. on July 3rd. Alisha hadn't been there today, nor Phil. He'd taken the handoff from Jeff, the manager, at 1:30, and it had been a quiet day since. There wasn't much chance of anything interesting going on the rest of the night. The city was dry, so Drug Barn lost business to stores half a mile away in the township, where everyone was now filling up on beer for the next day. A slow drip of customers trickled in, fast food workers getting cigarettes on their way to the late shift at Taco Bell, a mother getting the store brand sun block that was on sale, kids from the apartments behind the store picking up ice cream to go with the video games they'd be playing for the next ten hours. Bill did the audit, took the deposit to the bank across the street, and felt the humid air vibrate around him as firecrackers popped from the apartments.

Fourth of July morning, Tony told Bill to go to the gym without him. It wasn't ideal to split up just a few days into their resolution, but it couldn't be helped. Tony was working the morning after the mid-shift, followed immediately by another pool party at his house. Bill couldn't go, though, because he had the store himself for the full thirteen hours that day in exchange for Jeff covering him later in the summer when Bill wanted to go to Motley Crue's final tour at Blossom Music Center.

Bill's workout that morning started out great. It was back day, which was probably the best day of the week to split up, as there weren't any lifts Bill needed a spotter for. The gym was nearly empty, and nobody detracted from his pulling one hundred pound dumbbells on his one-arm bent rows. He wrote one set neatly in his green book, waited his ninety seconds seated on the bench listening to "Enter Sandman," did his next set and wrote it again.

On his last heavy set, he decided to go to 110 pounds. He was feeling good. This was a great idea of Tony's. To start over with a new purpose in mid-year. Not just mid-year. While twenty-six wasn't really mid-life, it felt like Bill was in the middle of something. He'd been one of the smartest kids in his high school. His grades didn't show it, but who minded grades? He'd done well when he wanted to, and everything that didn't interest him, he figured he'd get to eventually. It had been a lot of fun to tell the honor roll kids how he'd beaten them on the SAT. He'd skipped college, saying he was tired of formal education, and besides, he could make 35K a year as an assistant manager at Drug Barn. Fifty thousand if he made manager.

Just out of high school, he told himself he made better money than a teacher. He'd stayed at home with his mother, a fact which he had actually tried to use as a selling point with the women who gave him their numbers. He'd already saved enough to pay cash for a house. He just needed the right woman to say when the time to leave had come. He felt it made him seem more serious.

But no matter how seriously he took himself, the women he dated seemed to see their relationships with him as for fun only. Bill was the goofy kid who hadn't grown up, the guy with all the muscles at the place where they bought tampons and Echinacea on the way to and from their grown-up office jobs. No matter how many books Bill could prove he'd read or how high a score he'd gotten on his SAT's, he was "a ten-fuck guy," as one girl had put it. After that, they laughed while they moved on, saying they didn't want to tie someone like him down. They didn't ask how he felt about being tied down. They moved down the road to buy what they needed to avoid running into him.

As Bill pulled the weight up on his sixth rep on his left side, he felt a slight twinge in the back of his upper shoulder. It wasn't terrible pain; he even finished the set. After he was done, it just felt a little tender, and it was hard for him to turn his head to the side. He had a few sets of pull-ups left, and he performed those, but took it just a little bit easy. He stayed in the shower for a few extra minutes, letting the hot water seep into it. He should have stretched longer. Still, it didn't seem too bad.

It bothered him a lot driving to work, as he had to spin around to check his blind spot along Main Street. The parking lot was a crucible. As soon as Bobbi opened her register, he bought a bottle of Advil and took four. He needed to keep moving. If he stopped, his neck would tighten up, and he'd never be able to loosen it up again. He couldn't afford to be beaten down by pain, not with a thirteen-hour day ahead of him.

Alisha wasn't there, so that was one less distraction. She'd asked off to be with her boyfriend. Bill had never met him; he'd only seen him dropping Alisha off in a pickup truck he'd once heard her say she'd paid for. Bill had heard her boyfriend, Lou or Larry or something, bawl at her from the cab to move her ass. But he doubted he was ever actually abusive—Alisha didn't seem the kind to put up with that. He took care of her son—Tony's son—who was in first grade and in the same elementary school Bill had gone to. Maybe Alisha figured that a man who didn't mind she had a kid was the best she could do. Bill had certainly never offered himself as an upgrade.

Bill tried to get a good start on rotating out the Fourth of July stock for back-to-school. He left a few sparklers in a small display by the checkout and moved the rest of the summer stock to the regular seasonal aisle, which cleared room on the extra display by the front door. He didn't like working by the front—customers had a habit of asking for things they could have otherwise found themselves if someone was there, and it interrupted his train of thought so often he made slow progress with changing out the display. Luke and Demani, two goofy high school kids, were his stock crew for the day. They were both only on until 3:30, and then were headed to picnics. He knew he wouldn't get much work out of them, so he made them a deal: get all the back-to-school stuff out of the back, and you can slack of the rest of the day as long as I don't see you.

They had it out by 11:30, and he was on his own with his thoughts. I should tell Alisha what I feel. She already has someone. I'm better. She might not think so. What if she did? Yes, what if? It's Tony's kid. He's the dad. Tony's like your brother. You want to date your brother's baby's mom?

He answered a call from the registers to approve an override. He walked with a customer who wanted to be shown exactly where the mousetraps from the ad were. He chased Luke and Demani back out of sight somewhere when he saw them throwing maxi-pads at each other in the aisle—a game they titled "rag tag." And when he got back to what he was doing, he had to start all over with the same thoughts from the beginning. The knot in his upper shoulder grew tighter and tighter. He took more Motrin. He got confused about where he was in reworking the display, and asked himself a new question: *what the fuck am I doing?* He didn't mean it in the larger sense, but the minute it came out of his mouth, it felt like it fit.

About six, the store was deserted. People were drunk at their cookouts and resting up for fireworks. There would be a rush at about eight for bug repellant and batteries for flashlights and sparklers as people headed to the football field for the city's display. Feeling a sudden spite he didn't understand, Bill moved the insect repellant from where it was by the front door to a place where nobody would find it. A text came in from Tony.

Bro, u shld come by after work. Great party.

Bill had planned to go straight home after work, play a few games of gin with his mother on the screened-in porch listening to the illegal fireworks go off. He had to open the store the next day.

Don't get off till ten. Will it still be going by then?

Yeah, man. Just come.

Bill didn't respond for an hour. Tony kept pinging him every fifteen minutes. Bill responded that he was having a problem with a customer. Five years ago, it would have felt natural to hang out with Tony all night, to hold firecrackers in his hands while he ran and jumped from the diving board, trying to see if he could get them to explode just as he was about to hit the water. But Bill felt out of place at Tony's with his wife and their baby and their house and their grown-up jobs and grown-up life.

Bill everyone here is saying they want you to come.

Bill rotated his shoulder, and thought it was finally loosening up. Why not? They had committed to renewing their bodies and their lives together, why not spend a few carefree late summer night hours in his backyard? He stopped by the store down the street in the township and picked up a six-pack of the same cheap beer they'd drunk together in high school when Tony's brother bought it for them.

When Bill rang the front door of Tony's house, the light on the front porch was off. It took over thirty seconds before the light flipped on. Jaimie came to the door in a t-shirt that looked like it had just been thrown on. Her eyes were puffy and didn't match the rest of her face, which had such tight skin it seemed she was being choked with Saran Wrap. Her sandy hair was pulled up in a ponytail.

"Bill, what are you doing here?"

"Well, Tony's been texting me for four hours telling me to come."

"But the party ended almost four hours ago."

Bill was about to apologize and back off the porch, saying Tony must have played a prank on him, when Tony appeared in the hallway behind Jaimie.

"Bill! Buddy! You came!" He sounded drunk.

Jaimie shot Bill a look like he had slipped Tony a rufie.

"Sorry, Jaime, I didn't know. He's been sending texts. He said everyone was waiting for me."

Tony bounded down the hallway and put his arm around Jaimie, who looked annoyed but didn't push him away. "You brought Lake Erie Malt! Man, that takes me back. What say we down 'em together?"

Jaimie softly spoke into Tony's ear, just loud enough for Bill to hear. "Babe, you have to go to work tomorrow, and you had enough already today."

"I don't have to go until tomorrow night. And Bill's here."

She shot Bill one more reproachful look. "Well, I'd better get to bed, then." She said. "One of us needs to be in shape to go when the baby wakes up tomorrow."

Tony pulled Bill down the hall, through the kitchen, and into the dining room, where he sat Bill down at the table. It was a table Bill hadn't seen before.

"Like it?" Tony asked, his meaty face red and jaunty. "It's cherry wood or some shit. I never knew that kind of thing mattered until we went to buy the fucker."

Tony plopped his first can of Lake Erie Malt on the table, but Bill found a coaster. "Man, why'd you tell me everyone wanted me to come here if the party was already over? You messing with me?"

Tony took three long gulps from his beer and didn't stop until he ran out of breath. He let out a deep, satisfied sigh when he put his can back down. "I needed to talk to you about something."

"We're supposed to be at the gym together tomorrow morning," Bill said, not touching his beer. "You could have talked to me then."

"Couldn't wait. Needed to talk to you now."

"So talk."

Tony pounded the rest of his beer and opened a second. "Oh, man. Did Jaimie and I get into it today."

Bill immediately squirmed in his seat when Tony mentioned Jaimie. He was afraid she was listening to them on the steps. He adjusted his beer to the dead center of the coaster. "What about?"

"Well, Alisha is always short of money, because she has a shitty job—no offense—and that loser she's with doesn't help with anything. So Mikey's in first grade this year, and he wants to take acting lessons, of all damn things. And he needs new shoes and a bunch of other things, because he keeps growing out of what he has. Anyhow, I gave her like three times her child support last month, and so I came up short on the mortgage. Jaimie found out today."

"So what do you need, Tony? You need money? Say the word."

"No, money's not a problem. This is just a temporary thing. I can work a few shifts of security at a bar in the township and be back on track. The problem is that shit like this keeps coming up, and Jaimie's getting sick of it. She wants me to quit giving Alisha so much money. But how can I? That's my kid, too. And he's a good kid."

"Yeah, he is," Bill agreed. He thought of how Alisha had once brought Mikey to work when she had no daycare, and he'd been in the store for four hours without Bill knowing until she took him to the employee rest room. "But what do you want me to do?"

"Look, I know this is hard for you, but I'm going to have to ask you to have some balls."

Bill was just about to pick up his beer, and put it back down again. "Come again?"

"Balls, Bill. I know you usually like to sit back and be all philosophical about shit, but I need you to have some balls. Specifically, I know you're nuts about Alisha. I know you always have been. Well here's the thing. She's into you, too, man. She's just been waiting for you to say something."

"I'm not into her. I mean, she's cute, but there are a lot of cute girls working for me. And that's the thing, Tony. She works for me. I can't date someone who…"

"Oh, come off it. Jeff was putting it to two different cashiers at once when we worked there. And he's still there."

"I don't want to be like Jeff."

"So don't. But don't pussy out over someone you've had a boner for since high school over some bullshit excuse."

"Look, man, she's cute, but it's not like I'm infatuated with her."

"Oh, man. You know the only reason I ever messed around with her was because I thought it would make you jealous enough to grow a pair. I was trying to be your wing man. Things just got a little out of control that day is all. We both got a little too high smoking weed in the stock room. The plan was to just get her interested enough for you to make your move."

Bill tried to make a casual move for his beer can, but miscalculated and knocked it over. Foam fizzed all over the wood, and a rivulet of beer made for the side, ready to head over the falls and onto the carpet. Bill looked frantically for a paper towel, a napkin, anything, but couldn't find one. He tried to use the bottom of his shirt."

"Leave it!" Tony ordered. It was his cop voice, his don't-mess-with-my-friend voice he used at the gym. Bill sat back down, and the beer made audible plinking noises on the white carpet.

"Look. You're my best friend. But Jaimie doesn't want you around, because she thinks you're a bum and irresponsible and possibly a bad influence. And I can't keep paying for Alisha's life and ours, too. So I need you to man up and take care of her. You'd be good to her. I'd be able to pay less, and you'd be couple friends with a kid, so you could come around more often. Hell, I'd even see more of Mikey. And then, I wouldn't have to worry about what kind of man is around him, because it'd be you."

Bill got up from the table. He said it was pretty clear that Tony was drunk, and since they were supposed to meet at the gym early the next day, he'd better get to bed now. As he passed through the hallway back to the front door, he thought he heard soft footsteps padding up the stairs.

When he woke up the next morning, Bill couldn't move his neck at all. Everything had turned to one great knot during the night. It took him several minutes to fight his way out of bed, keeping his left side still and pushing with his right arm. He had to ask his mother to drive him to work, which she did, and gave him a Percocet from her medicine cabinet. She also called at eight and got him in at Dr. Spitzer's at noon. He would open the store, survive a few hours, then leave his keys with the head cashier. A few hours with no manager wouldn't leave the place to burn down.

But Phil was there before the store even opened. He had six stores under him; why was this store the one he always seemed to come to? Phil wanted to change everything about the back-to-school display Bill had worked on the whole day before. If Phil noticed how gingerly Bill moved, how he winced every time he raised so much as a pack of mechanical pencils, Phil didn't say anything.

Alisha did. When Phil asked where the insect repellant had

gotten to, Bill had to retrieve it from behind the display of defective make-up where he'd hidden it, and he passed Alisha on the way.

"What happened to you?" she asked. She didn't have her usual playful tone.

"Hurt it lifting yesterday."

She only nodded her head and went back to work without comment.

After a few hours of torment, Phil unexpectedly started to leave around lunch time. Bill was relieved, because he didn't want to have to explain to Phil that he had to leave the store for the doctor. Just as Phil was headed toward the exit, he snapped his fingers and turned to Bill. "Oh, almost forgot. The store in New Philly is a done deal if you want it, and I assume you do."

Bill had a look of fake surprise in his repertoire, but his neck wouldn't allow it. He was about to opt for simply saying "Yes, I'd love it, thanks very much," but the split second it had taken him to shift from one gesture to the other had triggered hesitation in him. He said he'd almost certainly love to, but he just had to check on it; the store was a long way away, he was worried about his mother (although her health was fine), and he'd know in a couple of days. Phil looked surprised, his bald forehead crinkling back. He said he'd already told corporate that Bill would take it, but never mind, it could wait until Monday.

Bill's mother arrived at 11:30. Alisha wished him well as he left. The doctor said it was a bad strain, and prescribed muscle relaxers and pain killers. He said that as Bill got closer to thirty and so on, he'd have to watch out more and more for these kinds of things, and that to prevent them, he'd have to take it a little easier. Bill explained that it was a resolution to get fit, to get strong, and wasn't that good for his health? But the doctor just looked bored and typed the prescription and looked at the screen.

"Should I send this to the Discount Drug Barn on Main Street? Oh, that's where you work, isn't it? That's convenient. Anyhow, everything in moderation."

Bill's mother took him back to the store and came inside with him while Bill handed off the store to Jeff. As soon as Bill rounded the check-out counters, he heard shouting coming from the far wall. Keeping his head as still as possible, he walked faster toward the commotion. When he had passed the Mason jar end cap, he knew it was coming from cosmetics.

"All I said was that I wanted bacon in it. I don't like it without bacon."

Bill was certain that those were the words, but they didn't make any sense.

"I'm at work," Alisha replied, in a much softer voice. Bill could see her now.

"What's that supposed to mean?" Lou or Larry bawled. He was wearing a blue dress shirt and a red striped tie that wasn't tucked all the way beneath his collar. "I'm looking, ain't I? Like you want? Got this damn tie on, don't I?"

"I'm at work," she softly replied again. Bill was next to Lou or Larry in front of the glass displays of perfume.

"Hey, man, this isn't the place for this conversation. You've got to take this someplace else."

"Hey, fuck you, you half-pint little fairy!" Lou or Larry shouted at Bill, and turned to him. His face was scorching orange-red, as much from tying his tie too tight as from anger. He was much taller than Bill, but that wasn't new. Normally, Bill would have had him in a full nelson in three seconds. But he couldn't move. The knot in his neck was throttling him, just like the tie was throttling Lou or Larry.

"Man, I'm going to need you to leave the store…"

Lou or Larry swung at Bill. It was a slow, clumsy swing, full of power but awkward. Bill moved to duck, but was slowed by his neck. The blow caught him in the shoulder, making his neck snap, which sent an agonizing pulse of pain through his head and back. He fell to the ground. He tried to jump back up, but had to first roll awkwardly to his right side to push himself up. When he staggered to his feet, he found that Lou or Larry was already lying on the ground, knocked out cold. Tony stood over him, and was pulling handcuffs from out of his back pocket.

Jeff arrived for his shift and told Bill to go home right away. Tony, while waiting for the backup he had called to come arrest Lou or Larry for assault, explained that he'd come because he was worried when Bill didn't show at the gym. He thought Bill had been angry about last night. Bill's mom filled his prescription at the pharmacist, brought him a bottle of water, and had him take one each of the pills. Alisha and Tony both helped Bill out to the parking lot and laid him down in the back of his mother's sedan. The pills began to hit, and Bill felt relief wash over him. Before Tony could pull himself back out of the car, Bill grabbed him by the arm and pulled him into a bear hug. He squeezed with all the force he had, with fury at Tony's infallibility, and gratitude for his loyalty. "I love you, you stupid bastard," he said.

"I'm not the one you need to tell," Tony said. "I already know."

Alisha disappeared, but then quickly came back and opened the back door. "Shit," she said. "Do you think you can ask your mom to take me home? Leo had the truck keys."

They rode silently in the back together, his mom chauffeuring like they were middle schoolers on their first date. Alisha sat against the window. He lay across the bench with his head in her lap. His mother was humming cheerfully along to her old Steely Dan CDs. His head bounced up and down on Alisha's thigh when they hit a pothole, and she put her hand on top of his head to steady him.

"I know that in the big picture of things, you're the one who had the worse day, today," Bill told her. "You should probably be the one lying down." She laughed, but said nothing.

Half asleep, he heard the car stop, and Alisha and his mom got out. Alisha's mother and Mikey were outside, and there were questions about whether Alisha was all right. His mother had left the car on, the air conditioning running. He curled up to keep warm and felt the corner of something hard poking his hand. It was his green journal. Blurry-eyed, he opened it with one hand and looked at the last page he had written in. The print was sideways from him as he was stretched across the seat. At the bottom of his last set of pull-ups, he had written a note. *Tweaked something.*

Hope it's not too bad. Below that, one thin sentence, in rounded letters that weren't his. *I've always known you were strong. I just want to know when you're going to be strong enough.*

He shot up in the car. His mother was listening as Alisha's son—Tony's son—sang a song he had learned in drama class. Bill felt at his left pectoral. Miraculously, his pen was still in his shirt pocket. He wrote hurriedly, trying to be legible, and finding that made it more difficult to write the letters straight. He ripped out a page and opened the car door. He slowly crept toward Alisha with his head tilted down.

Her mouth started to form a question, but he pushed the note into her hands and returned to the car. "Hey, Mikey. I'll see you later."

He was asleep before they pulled out of the driveway. He stirred only slightly as he was tossed in the back by the familiar turns of his home town. His mother, no longer listening to her music, still hummed pieces of it. *They got a name for the winners in the world, I want a name when I lose.* That was how that part of it went. Was that what he had written in the note? No, it was something else. "Phil offered me my own store, but I want to know what you think." He had put something else in as a post-script. Or he had meant it as a post-script, but then when he wrote it, it felt like that was the main part of the message. He remembered that handing her what he'd written felt like passing notes in study hall. *I don't even know what strong means,* he had written. God, how he'd love to see her face when she read it. How he'd love to see her face.

Dogs and Days Don't Wait to Be Called

Hiwet couldn't say how long she had been pregnant when the aid worker's words were relayed to her through the interpreter. Hiwet said it had been a week since she could remember throwing up, then waited while her words passed from interpreter to nurse, emerging as sounds that meant no more to her than bird song. The interpreter had a forehead that seemed to bulge outwards, making it seem like her eyes were looking down at her own face. She had a habit of beginning her translation while Hiwet was still in the middle of speaking, leading Hiwet to wonder if she was getting it all. The nurse was pale with a patina of grease and fatigue; she had two-tone skin with sunspots, a protruding nose and pointed ears, and reminded Hiwet of a hyena. The interpreter finished delivering Hiwet's message, and the nurse puckered her lips over her teeth far enough to reveal gums. It was an expression that meant *there isn't much time to make a decision*.

As a girl in Eritrea, Hiwet had seen red spitting cobras on a few occasions. If her brother was around, he threw rocks at them until he landed enough to render them harmless. Once they stopped moving, he then cut off their heads with a hoe and left the body for the street dogs and buzzards of Tesseney to eat. A cobra once got far enough to lunge at one of the family chickens. Somehow, the chicken jumped out of its way and scurried to safety. It was one of the same chickens she fed every day, too dumb and slow usually to get out of the way when she kicked it back from the gate. But when the snake had gone for it, so quick and deadly that even Hiwet had barely seen the flash of movement, the chicken instantly reacted with life-saving agility.

So why had Hiwet's reaction to the Rashaida who'd raped her been only useless cringing and whimpering, a denial and a resignation at once? The men who held her for two months in the Sinai desert after intercepting her flight from Eritrea and slow starvation wore red turbans. Between their turbans and the white dish-dash, all that showed of them was the strip of dark skin from neck to forehead. The first had been so gentle when he took her to his tent from the cave where the other prisoners were held, she thought he was letting her know her family had paid the ransom and she could go. He struck suddenly, so suddenly she did not even realize he had stopped being gentle. She felt like a rat already paralyzed by poison, waiting to be swallowed.

"I can give you a few minutes to decide what you want to do," the aid worker told her, already standing up to leave, "but you have to decide now. Any longer, and you'll be too far along to end the pregnancy." She left, and the interpreter hurried to finish her work so she could run after the nurse. The interpreter guessed that Hiwet had maybe half an hour before the nurse would come back and need a decision.

Dogs were not pets in Eritrea. She had seen stories in newspapers about singers in America who cared for their little dogs like babies, carrying them around in tiny bags, bedecking them with jewelry. In Eritrea, dogs either figured out how to get along on their own or they died. But while Hiwet's family got hungrier and hungrier, there seemed to be always more and more dogs on the streets. The chickens were sold, and her family existed on grim weekly provisions of sorghum. The dogs had no social programs. Yet they ate, they bred, they survived.

The boat had capsized half a mile off the coast of Lampedusa. She'd never swum a stroke in her life, but found she could do it when she had to. It had cost her family twenty thousand dollars to get her away from the Rashaida, across Sudan, into Libya, and into that leaking tub that set out to cross the Mediterranean. Her brother threw a dog into a river once. The dog had probably never swum in its life, either, but it figured it out.

Dogs, chickens, snakes. Humans. Only a human would think itself to death with speculation when faced with hungry fangs. Only a human would consider not allowing the little version of itself developing inside a womb to keep developing. She should be more like a chicken or dog, just act on the blind instinct to live, dive forward. "Dogs and days don't wait to be called," a saying of her father's went. It meant that time marched on whether you wanted it to or not, but it also meant that dogs didn't care that they weren't wanted. No harm in just showing up and seeing if there was something to eat.

The nurse would not wait to be called. She would be back soon, needing an answer. But where to find such an answer? She thought of church: the celebration of *Timqet*: bright colors, parades, umbrellas, the replica Ark of the Covenant walked through the streets. Incense. Chanting. Some things are sins. Some things are good. Some things, it depends. She thought she had heard of abortion—once—as a very bad thing done in America. Nobody had ever asked a priest what the right thing to do was if kidnappers had impregnated you against your will, robbed you of your faith in God, then left you to go live as a beggar in a strange land. To ask a question like that, one that supposed God could make a world where such things could even happen, would be like spitting on the Ark.

After ten minutes of waiting for the nurse to return, Hiwet would have said she would let the little version of herself keep growing inside of her until it was ready to come out into the world on its own. Turn the worst thing in her life into something good. Spin poison into mother's milk, that kind of thing. But in minutes eleven through twenty-three, she tried to think of the men who might be the father of the little version of herself. It would be a little version of one of them, too. She didn't know for sure how many there were. The cobra had been the first, but then there was the ugly one—a captor so deformed, even the other Rashaida made fun of him. After the ugly one was the handsome one. Hiwet had time to wonder why he was raping girls in the Sinai, when he could have been charming them on television. There was a man whose face she never saw, because he took her from behind, like a dog, and then left. After that, she didn't notice anything about the men anymore.

She didn't know what would become of her in the next six months. She didn't know how she would live. She didn't know if she would be sent back to Eritrea, where she'd probably be sent to prison. There had been talk that Europe was changing its tune on refugees. They had too many to feed already. Too many people in the life boat sinks the whole boat, and everyone drowns. Why would she bring a baby onto her sinking raft, only to go down together?

She heard the nurse's voice like water and the interpreter's like gravel through the curtain that separated her from the next patient. The nurse would not wait to be called. Every decision Hiwet had made that mattered was one she had been forced to make quickly, based on one choice after another she didn't think she knew how to make. There was no work in Eritrea. There was nothing to eat in Eritrea. There were too many people to care for in her family. She had been due to enter the military school at Sawa. Some said she would only be in the military for a year and a half. Some said the government would keep her until she was too old to work. There was a man she knew who said he could get her across the border into Sudan and on her way to Israel or Europe for ten thousand Nakfa. Some said life was better outside, even if you ended up cleaning toilets in Saudi Arabia.

Some spoke of family who had been captured by the Rashaida while passing through the desert, then tortured to make the families willing to pay more and faster.

Her parents had offered her proverbs, but the proverbs contradicted each other. Her father, who fought the Ethiopians to make Eritrea its own country, said things like *you cannot call the forest you live in a jungle.* He knew life was bad, but he thought she could manage. He talked of when he was young, and *bread was like rocks.* He called her dreams of leaving "chicken's dreams," idle thoughts.

But her mother riffed off the chicken. *Eventually, the egg will grow legs and walk.* Also, *save your chicken before it starts flapping*. Go while you can, save yourself. Everything contradicted something else. Yes and no were equally balanced, and the only judge to arbitrate between them was Hiwet. But Hiwet didn't know the answers. Solomon lay with the Queen of Sheba and God gave the Ark of the Covenant to Sheba's child to take to Eritrea to keep safe, which the Church had done for thousands of years. So why did she have no wisdom to choose? Anyway, Solomon had decided between two women who both wanted the same baby. How to choose between one woman who wanted to keep the little version of herself and one who didn't, when those two women were part of the same person?

Every adage she had learned was in violation of some other adage. The one she could think of that had to do with having children even seemed to violate itself. *The cow gave birth to fire. She tried to lick the fire. She burned her tongue and tried to leave, but she couldn't because the fire was her child.* So, a mother hates the little version of herself, but really has no choice in the matter, so she loves what she hates?

The nurse was entering the room again, along with the interpreter. Both looked even more exhausted now than they had thirty minutes ago, the grease from their faces seeming to have leached into their eyes from rubbing. They would want an answer. Keep the little slithering person, the venom that leaked from some snake in the Sinai growing inside her, or smash its head with a rock?

The need for an answer was relayed from nurse to interpreter, then from interpreter to Hiwet. She was out of time to think. Dogs and days don't wait to be called. Neither do chickens or snakes or cows or human smugglers or kidnappers or governments. Hiwet gave no answer, and the nurse thought she had not understood. She softly stepped toward Hiwet and put a small hand on her abdomen. "Keep? Don't keep? It's hard, I understand."

Hiwet tried to think of whether her parents had ever shown any sign of being glad they had brought her or her sisters and brothers into the world. Not her father, she thought. He was all thin arms and legs that whipped around when he reached for a can of kerosene or crossed his legs on the one ancient chair the family owned. He had never willed his arms to hold her. She couldn't imagine how someone so skinny had once carried a heavy machine gun when he fought the Ethiopians. His limbs seemed to control him. He had no choices to make; he was simply the slave of a will that moved him. His only choice was to endure the fate his limbs subjected him to.

Her mother was full of phrases that indicated her devotion. *B'ruhti kuni, gualey.* Be blessed, my daughter. Her mother seldom ate because her children needed to eat first. When she did eat, *injerra* seemed to stick in her dry throat; the pauses between bites were chasmal. She wanted her children to dance on festival days, but did not dance herself. She seemed content with Hiwet's decision to leave, and gave her a gold bracelet and silk cloth that the Rashaida then took from her.

"Keep or don't keep?" the nurse asked again, and slid her arm across Hiwet's abdomen and up, onto her shoulder. Her white smock was emblazoned with a bright red stick human figure surrounded by horizontal red stripes, the symbol of the aid agency. Her eyes were watery with a delta of capillaries flaring. She looked sick to her stomach, exhausted and engorged from empathic consumption of human misery, but ready to vomit it all up to swallow more.

Her arm moved from Hiwet's shoulder to touch her cheek, but Hiwet swiped it away. She reached for the nurse's eyes and tried to claw at them. The woman screamed, a squashed, bleating trumpet honk drowned out by the sound of two dozen screaming, hungry babies in the tent. The nurse and the interpreter struggled to loosen Hiwet's grasp on the nurse. "*Gualey! Intay t'gebri zelebi?* What are you doing, my daughter?"

At last, Hiwet's nails came lose and the nurse ran from the room, only a small red mark showing on her cheek as she turned to go. Hiwet found whatever she could find loose in the room, a dull pencil and a notebook, and threw them after the nurse. The notebook flapped to the ground like a flightless bird. Hiwet licked the fire of her own rage as her one chance to choose something else fled out the tent and into the mild Mediterranean winter.

About the Author

Jacob Weber is a translator living in Maryland. He has been a Marine, a retail clerk and manager, a waiter at a Korean restaurant, and a volunteer mentor and English tutor to immigrant adult learners. He is currently a fiction reader for *The Baltimore Review*. Like nearly everyone living in the D.C. region, Jacob is from Ohio, where he graduated from Walsh University after his enlistment in the Marine Corps. He has an M.A. in English with a concentration in creative writing from the University of Illinois at Chicago. He has written a novel on the adventures of a translator of a pretend language for a government agency. He blogs about workshops, fiction, doubt, rejection, why the *Lord of the Rings* movies make him angry, and whether fiction is really good for you at workshopheretic.blogspot.com.

CPSIA information can be obtained
at www.ICGtesting.com
Printed in the USA
FSOW01n1031080717
36136FS